Perfection "CAN" Be Had!

Also by Bernhard Dohrmann

Money Magic

Super Achievers

Diamond Heart

Redemption - How to Prosper in the Terror Economy

Published by Life Success Academy

200 Lime Quarry Road

Madison, Alabama 35758

1-890465-00-3

Perfection "CAN" Be Had!

My Father's Stories

Bernhard Dohrmann

as told from the scrolls of

Brother Al Dela Rosa

For Lynn

Contents

Part 2 - The Tall Ships

Part 3 - The Dohrmann Legacy

Foreword

➽ I can still remember what I felt like the first time I saw a bookstore with *Chicken Soup for the Soul*, with my name on the cover, in large display racks outside not one, but almost every major bookstore in the world. I can remember what the feelings were like when USA TODAY and my hometown paper both reported how many weeks *A 3rd Serving of Chicken Soup* had remained on the NEW YORK TIMES Best-Seller List, and how fast it had risen to number one.

It felt GOOD! Very, VERY GOOD!

As a bestselling author, I receive many requests for endorsements and I have taken great care in choosing which books I will endorse, especially in the rare moments when I "step inside" a new book and write a foreward. This care is part of the "quality control" I wish to make to my many millions of *Chicken Soup* readers.

I want my readers to know that one reason I chose to write a foreward for Berny's book is that I see the book as more "healing soup" for millions of readers. *My Father's Stories (Perfection Can Be Had),* like *Chicken Soup for the Soul,* features many stories, each appealing to different emotions and each teaching different and valuable life lessons.

Another reason I encourage you to read this book is part of my own individual story. For many years I have had the privilege to "learn" powerful lessons taught as *My Father's Stories* by Bernhard Dohrmann. These stores have touched my life. I have also watched these stories touch the lives of many thousands of others over the years. As a result, I feel the healing power contained in these messages deserves a wide readership.

The reader should know that I never met Alan Dohrmann when he was alive, although I often feel that in some magical manner he has adopted me and mentored me for a long while. I have known or know of many of the people who were Alan Dohrmann's students - the late Val Van de Wall, Tom Willhite, William Penn Patrick, Alexander Everett, Earl Nightingale, Dr. Edward Deming, John Hanley and Walt Disney to name only a few. I have also had the honor to know Jane Willhite with whom Alan Dohrmann worked for so many years, and through her eyes have gained a bit more insight into this

erfection
"CAN" Be Had!

special teacher.

I have primarily been able to know Alan Dohrmann and his work through the eyes of his oldest son, Bernhard Dohrmann, with whom I have taught many powerful personal development seminars. Over the past five years I have tasted the words of Alan Dohrmann as if he were still teaching them himself. If ever you have an opportunity to hear the spoken stories, do not hesitate to make a date with destiny! If Bernhard Dohrmann is teaching live, cancel other plans and make it a point to attend the lecture. You'll find it one of the most unique experiences of your life.

I never knew the author, Brother Al Dela Rosa, the Benedictine Monk who brings each story to life once again, although I know various members of the Dohrmann family, and subsequently I have a closer context for the stories you are about to enjoy. I know enough of the history, to know that even though *My Father's Stories* is labeled a work of fiction, much of the "story" is based on the real life experiences of the Dohrmann family.

Perhaps the cornerstone reason I want you to read this book is simply to invite you to return to the lost innocence of your own childhood. My partner, Mark Victor Hansen, and I believe in our hearts that the world needs a new *Alice in Wonderland* adventure, to take us all collectively and each individually into the twenty-first century.

In the end, it might be only through the eyes of the magical child that hides just beneath the surface in all of us that we once again rebirth our own connection to the miracles taking place all around us. *My Father's Stories* is above all, an adventure - a magical safari into the inner reaches of the heart, that compels the reader to return to what is most heroic within us - the child who is always the hero.

As you hear the words, see the colors, feel the heart throb, and embrace the magic one more time, the natural child in your own heart is likely to be re-awakened. For some it may only be for a moment in time, but like any fairy tale, a precious memory that lasts for an entire lifetime.

For others, this book may become a fork in your life's journey. It is for you, that I write this foreward.

My hope is to leave a simple fingerprint upon your soul. My request is that you embrace *My Father's Stories*.

Own each story through the "inner" eye of your childhood imagination. Allow each miracle, each message to reside at the deepest level of your own heart.

erfection
"CAN" Be Had!

As I close, my wish is that *My Father's Stories* be told and retold by the adult readers to the children of the world for generations to come. If this special dream for the *Perfection Can Be Had* stories becomes reality for the children of the world, then, like the loaves shared by a simple carpenter's son two thousand years ago, it will feed the entire world with abundance and love.

Your work is to serve the loaves!

Jack Canfield

Author, *Chicken Soup for the Soul*

Santa Barbara, California

Introduction

⚡ "If you can dream it, you can do it!" I often tell others in my leadership training seminars. With the emergence of this book, I am realizing one of my own dreams. My father, Alan Dohrmann, will always be my greatest hero, and all my life, I have dreamed about writing books that would bring forth his famous "lessons."

Anyone who knew Alan Dohrmann, or who was fortunate enough to attend one of his seminars, was quick to realize that he was an extraordinary individual with a unique and unforgettable style. As one of the founders of the human potential movement in this country, he was not only the wave of the future, he was the future.

The virtues and values that are the backbone of his training sessions (as well as the meat, vegetables and potatoes for his nine children during the growing years) are the same spiritual lessons upon which our great country was founded. With this book, I am stepping into my father's shoes and gathering all of you around me as my "family." I am also donning the robes of a dear and wonderful man, Brother Al

Dela Rosa, a Benedictine monk in the Catholic church, who was one of my father's closest friends and who became the godfather to my oldest son, Tony.

"Brother Al," as he was fondly called, was a frequent visitor at the Dohrmann homestead in Marin County. He spent most of his life never speaking a word, living under the sacred vow of silence. No one ever visited Montclair Abbey, the cloistered Benedictine monastery located on a high mountain in California, where Brother Al lived. The monks had no contact with the outside world, and no one spoke a word except in chant.

However, at one time, Brother Al was granted permission to leave the Abbey to receive special instruction from my father. A magical relationship formed between the two, and over time with the rest of the family as well, as he became a frequent guest in The Apartments of our Fairfax estate. In the family album are photos of my father, sporting a wide-brimmed hat and smoking a pipe. Standing beside him is a little man wearing the traditional long flowing robes of the Benedictine order. One photo, especially captivating to my children, is of myself sitting in Brother Dela Rosa's lap, gazing up as if listening to a story too sacred to turn away from, in order to please the photographer.

In 1993, several years after Brother Al's passing or "transition" – graduation, we like to call it — the Abbey forwarded a large trunk to me. Inside was a letter from Brother Al that explained the contents:

Dear Bee ("Bee" was my family nickname from childhood):

When Mr. Dohrmann was moving forward during his last lesson with you, he asked that I consider taking time to record what I felt were the most important of his lessons to the family. You will find over 1,000 scrolls which seek to address the promise I made to him in that final hour . . .

As you can see, these scrolls fill an entire chest. It is too much for one publication, but perhaps the world would enjoy them in some sequence.

I am reasonably certain that as the world comes to know your father, they will also remember much about their own greater family, as they may return again to the truth of being children in our world family once again.

However, that is not the lesson. (Can you feel me smiling with your father as you read these words?)

The lesson is, that these scrolls, my son, are for you and your children. . . for these are your stories . . .

I love you FOREVER

Brother Al . . .

Brother Al penned these scrolls with a monk's original quill. In the preface to these magnificent journals, he wrote:

Over a period of thirty years, I made more than three hundred personal visits to the Dohrmann estate, and each of these occasions was just as magical. Most of all, I looked forward to the lessons, to these special evenings when Mr. Dohrmann would hold forth.

After the children grew and had their own children, he would continue to teach them, and always in the same fashion, through the ancient and powerful means of stories told in the circle.

I can remember Thanksgiving and Christmas holidays when almost fifty of the "marrieds" as he liked to call them, and their children, would arrive. Even in those times, and in the late 70s, when he was failing in his health, it was the same. There was always the piano concert first, and always the special props and lessons told in an unforgettable way. Lessons reserved for "the children."

And there was always the tradition. The original nine children sat first in a semicircle on the floor before the large easy chair. The "youngers" would then sit in front of them, in their own easy circles. The "babies," whose attention was apt to wander, were retired to a family playroom. They didn't like that, of course, because they certainly didn't want to miss out on all the action. It was a special moment in their lives, as significant as an initiation or rite of passage, when a "baby" was deemed old enough to join the rest of the family and be part of *The Lessons*.

I have been told by the children that I am the only remaining person that has the content of the stories in such a condition so as to render a worthy publication. They do not know whether the world will treasure the tales as they unfold, but it matters only to me, for the legacy of Mr. Dohrmann, and five girls and four boys, that the stories are recorded.

Should they entertain you, that is sufficient. Should they move you to future courses of action, we have a miracle. Should they move someone you love to find a better way through life, we have a completion . . . a completion to my life, and to each reader so benefited.

There is a "belonging" to these lessons. Certain stories seem to find just the person that requires them most, just at the moment they require that particular story most. Hearing such a story, one that seems tailored exactly to your needs of the moment, is like finding a treasure chest on some magic beach. The sand is white. The breeze is warm and gentle. There is no other living creature to distract you. Not even the nearby waves render enough movement to take your gaze from the jewels that await you.

It is as if once you lift the lid of life, there is no disappointment. The jewels are really and truly there. Each is bright and perfect enough with its own divine beauty to satisfy your hunger for a thousand lifetimes.

〰〰 Some would say that I was luckier than most because I was born into a family of wealth and position. I would disagree. Although I never knew hardship during my growing years, I soon learned that, regardless of our race, religion, background or circumstance, each of us still has to forge our own frontiers. We still have to learn to integrate those intrinsic values that build character and mold a destiny with a purpose. And we still have to learn how to "visioneer" in order to make our dreams come true.

The Dohrmann story began in Germany, where my great-great-great-grandfather was a Baron who was assigned to the Royal Court as the Surgeon General to the King of Denmark. At the age of seventeen, the eldest Dohrmann son decided to cross the ocean and strike out on his own. I'm sure he believed this adventure in the New World was going to be much fun and not a lot of work. After all, could the sheltered genteel life of a nobility be much different in America from what he had experienced in Europe?

The first Law he learned on the ship, even before setting foot on American soil, was The Law of Leveling – a Fact of Reality that is the heart and soul of democracy. Nobility, titles, and royal lineage meant little to the frontier people. They had a different set of measurements for determining a person's "salt." A person was measured not for what was inherited, but for what was inherent. Those intrinsic values included courage, honesty, integrity, self-reliance, generosity, resourcefulness, commitment to and practice of the Golden Rule, thriftiness, industriousness . . . You know the list as well as I do.

The young Dohrmann who ventured across the ocean on his own soon learned that there is no room in this New World for anyone who thinks that happiness, abundance and the good life are going to be delivered on a silver platter. This didn't stop him, however. With gusto, he rolled up his shirt sleeves and set to work. The Dohrmann Empire – the Emporium stores and Dohrmann Hotel Supply, were the fruits of his labor, and his children and children's children reaped the benefits.

By far, the most important treasure that was passed down through the Dohrmann lineage were my father's teachings. These "lessons" became the watchword of my life and the lives of millions of others who attended his courses and workshops or hired him as their personal coach and trainer. The list of those who benefited from Alan Dohrmann's trainings is long and impressive, including Walt Disney, Napoleon Hill, Dr. Edward Deming, Alexander Everett, Bill Dempsey, Clement Stone, Warner Erhardt, and many others.

In today's high-tech, high-stress world of early burnout and what's-the-use syndromes, these lessons are intended to serve as an inspiration to those who share my passion for preserving the authentic experience and values of Family and Family Life. It is my hope and dream that all of you will become "runners" who will carry these lessons with you wherever you go, just as I have done; and that you, too, will share them with your friends and family.

Part 1

Golden Nuggets

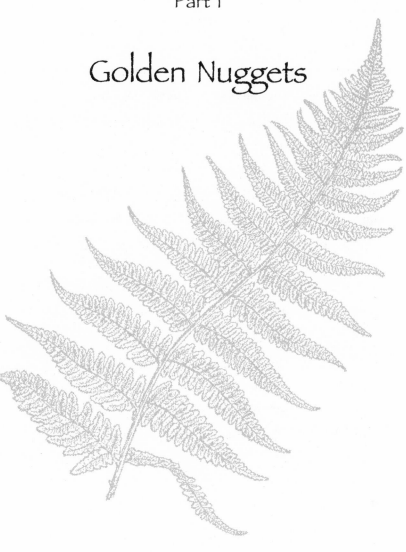

The Gingerbread House

⬛ The way it was told that night, it was really Ricky Brown's fault. It seems that yesterday afternoon he had wandered over to the Dohrmann estate, opened the large iron gates, and in spite of the household staff's disapproving frowns, ventured down the terraced walkways to the play area. Not that it was unusual for eight-year-old Ricky to arrive unannounced. It was his custom. After all, he was the leader of the pack of playmates, and leaders had special privileges — didn't they?

Ricky Brown lived down Bothine Drive, right at the end of Old Bay Road. The rest of the pack included four-year-old Bernhard "Bee" Dohrmann, the youngest (Bernhard could not pronounce his own name in those early years so he had been labeled by the family for what he COULD pronounce. From age two, the first-born son had been known simply as BEE. Even now, when "Bee" is nearly fifty years old, the family still affectionately calls him by this name, and he is "Grandpa Bee" to the grandchildren) . . . and the Tobin boys, Doug and Robin. The long winding front driveway of the Dohrmann estate ended almost directly across from the Tobin estate.

The Dohrmanns lived at 555 Olema Drive in Marin County. Alan Dohrmann, Bee's father, had originally purchased the estate as a summer home, but in 1952 he moved the family here permanently from the main homestead in the heart of San Francisco where four generations of Dorhmanns had played a prominent role in this famous city's development. The name "Dohrmann" on the West Coast was comparable to Mellon or Rockefeller in the East.

The play area, located out and above the Dohrmann main kitchens, was a magnet for all the neighborhood children. Surrounded by a circle of flowerbeds were swing sets, sandboxes, games, merry-go-rounds and spring-rider horses. The Dohrmanns kept the equipment in top working order. That was part of its attraction for the children, since the colorful, freshly painted equipment always made it seem like it was brand new. In fact, the play area was so popular, it had become more like a community park than a private family recreation spot.

Six-year-old Doug Tobin, Bee's closest friend, had already arrived and was playing with a group of older neighborhood boys, led by Larry Piambo. The Piambo family owned a huge estate adjacent to the Dohrmann home. On one part of the spacious grounds was an outdoor picnic area where the Piambo's would entertain as many as 500 Shriners. During these events, the children would often act as Indian Scouts, making raids on the huge mounds of fried chicken and delectable array of desserts.

Today, however, the boys were not stopping at the Dohrmanns', and no Piambo picnic raids were on the agenda. On this warm, early Wednesday afternoon in the summer of nineteen hundred and fifty-two, the pack was headed for The Forbidden Forest.

In order to get there, you had to walk across the Dohrmann grounds, through the double-lined walkways of flowers, past the vegetable garden, in between the lath house and compost pile, and out the back way, through the barbed-wire fence to the trail. Once you got to the trail, you would climb one of the three giant stones called The Boulders, that sat like border guards to the long, sloping field beyond.

Here, to the right of the trail, was the Piambo mansion, planted like an ancient watch tower amidst the giant redwoods. Bee and the rest already knew it wasn't easy to get beyond this bastion. First you had to check on old man Piambo, to see if he was out working in the greenhouse, or his vegetable or flower gardens.

Old man Piambo had built the mansion with funds from the large, well-known California construction company that bore his name. Although he had retired several years ago and his sons actually ran Piambo Construction, he was still treated with old style Italian respect as the Don of Dons in his empire. Old man Piambo loved his grandchildren, of which Larry was the youngest. However, he believed strongly that all children should be SEEN, but never HEARD. In broken English, he could set any trespassing child into flight with a single word in Italian . . . one that required no translation.

The Piambo Estate was the last bastion before the freedom trail that led to the forests beyond. Once the lookout party gave the signal that the trail was "clear," the whole party would run in single file like an army platoon, to the large chain-link gate at the bottom of the long, sloping field.

Ricky had one of the lookout scouts assigned to hold the barbed wire as the younger ones scampered through to the trail. The older boys were already up on the tallest of The Boulders, taking stock of the Old Man Piambo situation. No sign, anywhere. The coast was clear. One of the lookout scouts plucked up a clean young blade of grass, placed it between his thumbs and blew the "safe" signal. The younger ones knew this sound and were ready to RUN!

Scooting past the long, wire fence of the Piambo vegetable garden on the right and the orchard further down the trail, breathlessly they made it to the double gates at the entrance. Bernhard and the rest of the younger scouts were small enough to squeeze through the binding chain, and off they scampered, across Old Manor Road. Once across the country road and past the stand of redwoods on the rising knoll, they ventured up the steeper trail that led to the forbidden forest.

The scouts knew it would be an ambitious climb, and today it would also be a hot one; but they were determined. The tall redwoods offered some relief from the blistering sun, for as they started their climb, soon they found themselves surrounded on all sides by these towering giants. Pools of shadows spilled out over the trail, and an occasional breeze riffled through the trees, fanning the air. Up they climbed, following the twists and turns of a trail that led them still higher.

Tiny monsters spread themselves from the upper boughs and teased the trail dust with weird images. Then there were the insect attacks, more a nuisance than anything else, but still, they had to be swatted at. Soon it became very quiet — and dark. The sun that until now was still winking through the trees, suddenly disappeared altogether.

At first the darkness was not foreboding because the end point still leaked light into the forest entrance. But then even this beacon disappeared and their only trail marker was the tall border of ferns.

Each footfall made a separate sound, softened and muffled by the dust and fallen needles. Surely they had entered into another time long ago, as ancient as these giant redwoods whose huge trunks rose above them in Gothic splendor. Each boy was remembering the stories they'd heard about these ancient trees. They had been present during all the wars of the past, and they were here even before the time when Jesus Christ was alive in the world.

Ricky suggested that each boy pick up a "magic stick" and strike the trees as they went. He said this act would protect the scouting party from known dangers of wood witches and the evil spells they might cast on young boys. Most of the party immediately complied, carefully selecting sticks to match their own height. Each was tested on a tall tree trunk for sound quality, and they discarded weaker sticks in favor of stronger ones with greater "power." These boys were veterans of the ancient forest . . . at least in theory.

The party wound its way upward through the delicate ferns and redwood giants, tapping the trees for luck and protection. No one in the group had asked for or given an explanation of why they were making this expedition or where it might end. On only a few occasions, they had tried earlier journeys that tested the way into these forests, but each of these attempts had terminated far short of the point where they lost sight of the entrance to the forest. Today they were exploring the REAL unknown, maybe even the time before Time itself!

After more than an hour of walking, the boys paused on a large stone outcropping to fill their belt canteens in the spring-fed stream that peeked out from the cool, mossy stones. Acquired from an army surplus store, the heavy metal containers were an important part of any major excursion for serious scouts.

As they paused by the stream and looked back from where they'd come, they felt their long journey into primitive times had already been accomplished. Still, going forward seemed more compelling when balanced against the prospect of returning downward along the now foreboding shadow line. It was already three o'clock and the sun had abruptly changed its angle of attack. Now it dipped just beyond the high mountain line, creating new shadows that instantly cast themselves like a scourge of demons, spreading into the remaining pockets of sunshine and devouring them.

Suddenly something moved among the ferns. "What was that?" A hand shot up. A tangible vibration. "Did you feel anything? Let's keep moving . . ."

"It's the witching hour," warned Ricky in hushed tones. "This is the time they're free to come out!"

"Yeah, and every tree must be tapped twice now if we're ever going to get out of here," whispered the usually fearless Doug Tobin.

"My magic is stronger than any old witches," chanted young Dohrmann loudly as he strolled with authority to the front of the pack. To reassert his claim, he tapped the trees on both sides of the path . . . right, left, right, left . . .

"If a four-year-old can take it . . .so can I," declared Brown, following Dohrmann's lead. Soon the youngest of the pack was way ahead of the rest, so far ahead, in the next instant, he disappeared over a rise in the trail. The others ran to catch up, and as they came to the top of the knoll and peered beyond, they noted for the first time that the trail sloped downward on the other side.

Young Dohrmann was twenty yards or so ahead, his hands woven into great four-inch squares of wire fence. The scouting party had found something! Ricky was certain it was the purpose of the entire mission.

▬▬ Bernhard placed a finger on his lips. "Shhhh!" he warned. The scouts scurried forward, knees low to the ground as they secured their own fence positions to the right and left of the youngest scout.

The wire squares seemed to go on forever, traveling along the uneven terrain and following contours way down in the valley and far above, on knolls beyond the outermost point of vision. Held in position by huge green posts, each open square formed a separate canvas, like a giant mural. It was as if the entire forest had been placed within a series of frames. And there, almost directly in front of them, yet still at a distance...

"What is it?" asked young Dohrmann.

"You're seeing what I'm seeing," declared Ricky. "You can

see what it is as plain as I can."

"Yeah," whispered Doug Tobin hoarsely. "It's all true. Every word of it. It's The Gingerbread House where they took Hansel and Gretel – for sure!"

His eyes widened. There it was, nestled in a grassy meadow, and if he put his face close to one of the wire fence frames, he could capture almost the whole of it in a single square!

The rest of the scouts lined up along the fence to see for themselves. Here was a whole new country, a storybook land indeed, with miles of trails inside the bastion of fence posts. Rock walls, terraces festooned with clumps of roses lined every inch of the trails, as if a bridal procession were soon to pass through. Every so often, pools of green lawn would interrupt the pattern, with groves of redwoods, from which hammocks swung back and forth in the gentle breeze.

"I could smell them before we got here," declared Ricky as if his personal authority had somehow been restored with that observation.

"Me too," seconded Doug Tobin.

"I could feel them," exclaimed young Dohrmann. The others looked at him strangely, wondering what he could have

meant by that remark. Then they all turned back once more
to gaze at the awesome vista.

Roses

~~~~ Showers of colors and scents filled the air. Bright reds, pinks, yellows, whites, even the rarest blues, greens, purples, blacks and burgundies . . . Every conceivable color and hue had been captured in the petals of the thousands upon thousands of roses in these glorious gardens. Some of the blooms formed elaborate borders around clusters of fruit trees. Others framed the soft green lawns through which terraced tiers of trails spiraled downward into to a single broad path. This rose-festooned walkway led directly to the porch and front door of the brown and green "gingerbread" home that sat squarely in the center of the garden. Even from the distance, the scouts could see that the carefully laid-out trails among the descending tiers of the symmetrical garden were sprinkled with fairy dust — magical drifts of fallen rose petals.

It might have ended there. The scouting party could have turned around and taken its secret back home, and that would have been the last of it.

But – how could they do that? Look at all those roses!

Roses . . . like the world has never seen.

So many.

So perfect.

And then, they spotted something else – something even more spectacular than the roses. Suddenly, their eyes swept in another direction.

The trail had come to an end, unless it was intended for hikers to climb or crawl under the wire fence – there were no gates. Once on the other side of the fence, however, there were many pathways that wound through the terrace of rose gardens and fern trees.

Among the tiers and stone embankments was one trail in particular that forked off to the left. This fork opened to a wider trail leading to a grove of tall ferns and three giant redwoods. Rising high above the cliffs and hills, these Sentinels were knitted together by one of the most amazing tree houses that had ever been constructed.

A TREE FORT!! They all spotted it at the same time.

It looked very old, like a frontier cabin or prairie house, and very inviting – far more inviting than just a rose garden.

"Get down!" ordered Ricky in his Full Command voice. "We've got to see if anyone is in there first! If no one is around, we can claim it as our fort of roses. It will belong to us!"

Ricky called the meeting to order. Was it "proper" to explore someone else's tree house, asked one of the older scouts. But then, argued Larry Piambo, a fence that was either very high or very long, to say nothing of being both, must have been put in place to keep people out — and keep people in.

Another of the older scouts reasoned that the fence might only be there to keep the deer from eating the roses. It seemed a bit extravagant that such a huge effort would have been made only for the purpose of keeping trespassers out.

"It's magic, pure and simple," Doug Tobin concluded confidently. "This fence was put here by magic."

"No one is going to argue with you, Dougie," agreed Ricky. "That's why we have our magic sticks, just for this kind of thing." He tapped his stick against the green fence post near him, and a loud dull thud echoed into the forest.

Young Dohrmann was already on his back, half-wiggled under the wire fence.

"What do you think you're doing?" Ricky hissed, standing over him and poking him with his magic stick.

"STOP THAT!" panted Dohrmann. "I know what I'm doing." His legs came free on the other side. "If you're smart, you'll follow me. The fence is not here to keep people out," he retorted. "It's here to keep children in." Dohrmann pointed his magic stick toward the gingerbread house. "If we use our magic sticks, we can always find our way back here, and the opening will appear if we tap it." The four-year-old's smile was so compelling, it warmed the others. Everyone knew truth when they heard it spoken.

Doug Tobin was the next to worm his way under the place where the wire bent back in just enough to make it possible... ..if you wiggled just right on your back . . . to make it up and under and into the garden. Triumphantly, Doug emerged, and then, slowly, all six managed to squirm and wriggle their way past the fence line. Each stood in silence waiting for the last one to cross over.

Crouching Indian-style, trained by Hopalong Cassidy and Roy Rogers, the party moved toward the big fork that led down to the tree house. They proceeded to the point where the roses started and then turned off to the wide trail on the left. This was the high trail, the one farthest from the Hansel and Gretel house below.

Circling far above the splashes of circular green lawns

and rock walls with the borders of rose gardens, finally they stood before the tree house. Now that they were standing directly below, it was even more inviting. Made out of barn wood, its moss-covered boards held the romance and adventure of another time. Here were rooms with quaint pitched roofs, rope-held stairways, and latched shutters above each of the six windows . . . The details were awesome.

Surely, these ancient wooden stairs had been made by pirates. They had even been fashioned after a ship's gangplank, for they were supported by huge ropes with rope-work banisters that lowered or raised them. The rope rails made it appear easy to race up or down the stairs, and little latches held open the large double doors open against the wind.

What should prevent them climbing those stairs?

Again, Ricky took up the lead and plunged ahead into the shadows of the open doors, disappearing inside the tree house.

"Hey, guys," he called out to the rest, who were still timidly standing at the foot of the gangway in the grotto of pine needles below, "you've got to see this. Hurry UP!"

The urgency in his tone was all the others needed. Without another moment of hesitation, they raced up the roped stairway and entered into the dark coolness within.

Inside the Tree House

🐾 The energy inside the tree house was so electric, it was literally crackling. Here was everything the young boys would ever hope for. Wordlessly, the group exchanged knowing glances. If their lives were to end this instant, it would not matter in the least. In fact it would be perfect, for with the discovery of the magic tree house, they were complete. Their young lives now had meaning.

The high-pitched roof gave a church-like, mystical feeling to being "inside." The group moved through the room, exploring the furnishings, their eyes wide with wonder and delight. Here was a miniature sink with real running water! And on the other side of the room was a table for snacks, and crayoning. In the center of the table was a vase of roses. Their fresh dewy fragrance filled the room. Carved into the table's surface was a four-color game board, laid out with oversize wooden, hand-carved checker pieces heavier than any they had ever seen before. On each side of the table were flaps that would make it much larger when they were unfolded and fastened in place.

As they looked down at the floorboards, the boys discovered to their amazement, even more board games down below, burned into the wood as if by witches' fire.

Little buckets of fruit sat off in the corners, as if waiting to be tasted.

Little towels were hung on little racks.

Against the far wall was a small treasure chest of still more games that spilled over onto the floor.

A sudden gust of wind swept through the open windows, tousling the curtains against the windowpanes. Outside, the large redwoods creaked and groaned like an old ship's planks straining against the sea. Puffballs of air raced along the floorboards as the house gently swayed back and forth.

"We're going to come back here over and over. You know that, don't you?" declared Dohrmann.

"Yeah, we know, we know," Ricky rested his chin on his arm at the windowsill and gazed out at the sea of roses below. He was feeling pretty good about his find. Probably no one else would have been able to lead the pack to an amazing tree house and millions of roses.

"We can bring stuff from home and make this place totally ours," Doug Tobin chimed in.

erfection
"CAN" Be Had!

"Wait, you guys . . .This tree house must have been built for other children. We're all going to get in trouble for just being here." Jeffrey Roberts put back the pieces to one of the board games he had been examining. He was thinking things he didn't want to think.

"Naah," Ricky waved his arms with authority. "LOOK at this place. It's old. Really old. And look." With his index finger he picked up some dust from the game table. "Any children who came to this place must be all grown up by now." That seemed to settle everything for Ricky. He scrunched back down once more to view the slopes of the rose garden and orchards to the valleys beyond.

Dohrmann wasn't so easily convinced. "What about those fresh roses on the table, Ricky? And what about that fruit? Who put THOSE in here if this place is so OLD?"

Lying flat on the floor to peer out through a knothole to the lower part of the garden, Doug Tobin, whose father was a lawyer, hissed, "If that IS the Gingerbread House, we won't have much time to get away if the witch comes out."

Ricky moved to the window for a better view of the house and poked his head out. "Well, if it IS the Gingerbread House, and if we hear even one sound, I want the entire scouting

20

party out of here like Flash Gordon. Everyone understand?"
He looked around at the group to make sure everyone was
nodding obediently.

And then it happened.

At first it was just a low-pitched howling, but it only took
a few short seconds to reach a crescendo that broke into fierce
insistent barks. Loud and growing louder. Non-stop.

The scouts had never heard any barking like it, ever before.
Surely this was a Dog from Hell, thought Dohrmann, who
had heard this phrase used once or twice before and didn't
exactly know what it meant until now.

The boys ran to the windows facing The Gingerbread
House, their eyes widening with terror as an enormous black-
and-white head appeared in the frame of one of the
Gingerbread House windows. Obviously, this Dog-Monster
knew who the boys were and where they could now be found.

The barking persisted. This was the sound of a demon dog
accusing the scouting party of a serious violation. At some
level each boy, now quaking with fear and a few visibly
shivering, knew that a wrong had been committed that would
require some form of retribution. This Hell Hound was huge
and powerful and cunning.

The walls of the tree house seemed to be narrowing and closing in. What was once a cozy, welcome hideout was rapidly transforming into a trap. As the barking persisted, each realized in the fullness of their dread that it wouldn't be long before they would be captured in their own tree fort by this fierce child-eating Monster.

And now, to their horror, they watched as the large green door on Gingerbread House slammed open so hard, its window panes shuddered. An oversized overfed black and white spaniel breathing fire, fangs fully bared, soared out through the door.

Then . . . exactly what they feared would happen next — The Witch appeared in the doorway!

The scouting party already knew she would be plump with short, cropped, gray hair that with its odd way of coming to points here and there, seemed to have been coifed by a butcher — or possibly a gardener with dull hedge clippers. Even the hat stuffed onto her head was pointed and mean-looking.

A grapefruit face squinted and strained in the direction of the tree house, then started down the main red brick walk that connected all the rose garden trails . . . and also led directly to the tree house.

The boys fell flat to the floor, peering out at The Wicked

Witch through the cracks and knotholes. So was THIS it? Was it all going to end here . . . just like Hansel . . . just like Gretel?

In the core of their being, each knew about this witch. There was no possibility for error.

And now the party of two, the barking Hell-Hound and Wicked Witch, began their slow approach. The Hell-Hound never left his Mistress's side, which the boys found rather remarkable. The Witch must be holding him in check with an invisible leash.

Snatching up a broomstick from a peg on the side of the house next to the one that had held her pointed hat, the Witch cried out in a voice that cracked with age: "Boys ... boys ... I can SEE you in there. I know you're up there. You can't fool me!" She pointed her broom handle directly at the tree fort and shook it vigorously. Surely she was casting spells, thought the boys. They could almost see the evil words leaping off the end of the broom handle.

"Boys, you'll hurt yourselves! You're too little and that's too high for you to play unsupervised. Now you come down here this minute or I'll have to come up there and get you out!" The Wicked Witch waved her broomstick threateningly and flung her arms in the air.

It didn't take much for the scouts to get the message. This witch needed no red brick walk to get her to where she wanted to go. They already knew she was about to board the broomstick and take off into the air in the direction of the tree house.

"She's not going to lock me in that old iron cage and eat me. I'm telling you, she's NOT going to eat ME!" shouted Ricky. Without another look behind at the rest of them, the brave leader flew down the trap door stairs, tore through the ferns and raced to the entrance of the Rose Garden.

The scouts no longer needed a witch for creating pandemonium. Everyone started to speak at once.

"I told you not to come into this place!" "I'm not sticking no bone out through a cage for the rest of MY life!" "You better come on, Bernhard!" "Ricky ain't seen a day when he can outrun me when I'm really, really scared." "Bernhard, ain't ya comin'?" "Do you think that demon dog can fly?" "Forget the dog, do you think SHE'LL fly after us all the way down?" "Don't forget your magic stick or we're doomed!"

"Bernhard, you better come now . . . You're the last one!"

Each cry was followed by footfalls like hooves at full gallop, as the little legs and shoes swallowed up the distance from the bottom of the rope-held stairs and down the paths toward the exit from the Rose Garden.

Back they raced, under the fence, through the forest and across the country road. "I wasn't really scared, you know." Ricky coughed and gasped for breath, waiting for the rest to catch up. "Me neither," the rest chimed in. "Hey!" Doug jerked his head around, in the direction of the forest. "Where's BERNHARD?"

Ricky followed Doug's gaze. The two stared into the deepening shadows of the forest. "Oh no," moaned Ricky. "Oh NO!" Silence fell over the group.

"He couldn't still be in the tree house." White-faced, Ricky turned his back on the forest trail. "We don't know which way he might have run. Bernhard didn't stay there, you all know that! You all KNOW that, right?" Everyone nodded. They all KNEW.

"He could have run ahead of us," Ricky swallowed hard. "He could even be home right now while we stopped to wait for each other. He's the one that's going to get in trouble."

Doug Tobin shook his head sorrowfully. "No one is going to believe us, you know. No one. We can't say we found a magic garden and a witch and the REAL Hansel and Gretel house.

We'd be grounded for weeks. Especially if the witch has already eaten Bernhard."

"Anyway, the Rose Garden probably wouldn't even be there for grownups," woefully added another. "It would be invisible to them. Like in Flash Gordon. It would drop out of time. Kids are probably the only ones who can see it, and go in . . . or out."

"Yeah, you're probably right," agreed Doug. "But what about Bernhard? He could be trapped up there with that old witch. Where is that going to leave all of US?"

"I'll tell you where it's going to leave all of US," exclaimed Ricky. "We're going to all face the music together. Each one of us is going to tell anyone, if they ask, and ONLY if they ask, the same story. And here's the story:

"One: We older ones went on a scouting party like we always do.

"Two: Bernhard was told he couldn't come, so he took a nap. We left Bernhard with instructions to wait and be our lookout at The Boulders 'til we got back — like he always DOES.

"Three: We got back to The Boulders and he was gone and we didn't know where he had gone off to. We called around but he was gone. We figured he went back inside to sleep.

"Four. So we just played in the children's yard until it was time to go home." Ricky swallowed hard and took a deep breath before continuing.

"Five: We don't KNOW what happened to Bernhard, and that's the TRUTH. We don't KNOW . . . so let's get on with it. That's IT. Everybody got it?" Ricky glared and stretched to his full height and then some, on tiptoe, to peer down over the group. He raised his hand, waiting for agreement.

The group nodded sadly, looking down at the ground. No one said a word. Ricky was already walking toward the big, double chain-linked gate toward The Boulders and back to the Dohrmanns. The rest followed slowly, as if by looking back and lingering, somehow the youngest member of the pack would leap out of the shadows. How wrong they were. No one appeared. For all they know, the ancient forest may have swallowed up Bernhard forever.

Alice Mahoney

As soon as the last boy had vanished beyond the line of green fence posts, the witch headed for the tree house. The monster dog galloped in frenzied circles around his mistress as if he were trying to break loose from his invisible leash. It was a good thing the witch was able to hold him back, thought Bernhard. Otherwise, who knows what he would do? A beast like that could storm the tree house head-on and devour a little boy in one large gulp and swallow, before that boy would even have a chance to ... The rest of the thought turned into an iceball and dropped into the pit of his stomach as once more the Hell Hound whipped away from his mistress and lunged toward the tree house.

"Please let her spell keep working," prayed Bernhard. At that moment, the witch turned her back on the tree house and replaced the broomstick on its peg. Terrified, Bernhard watched the witch's skirt whirl through the door of the Gingerbread House and disappear with the rest of her into the darkness of the interior.

The witch's departure only seemed to enrage the Hell-Hound even more. Barking and tearing at the air, now it lurched off its front feet and leaped with only its back feet in place, as if to demonstrate the impossible strain of the witch's tether. It was fierce all right; and dogs had a good sense of smell. Probably it was already licking its chops.

Bernhard curled up in a ball underneath the game table, holding his head in both hands. Even though this wasn't the same as a nuclear blast, he had a feeling that somehow those instructions, delivered to him by his older brothers and sisters, would fit just as well for this catastrophe. Surely the witch would soon re-emerge from the house with an iron cage. Or maybe she would use magic, and simply cast a spell over him, then carry his limp body to its final place of torment.

All of this was even more distressing when Bernhard thought about Ricky, Dougie and the rest of his "friends." They had escaped. Simply run off without him. No one had seemed to notice, or even care that they'd left him behind . . . alone... ..the youngest, left to die. OR MAYBE SOMETHING EVEN WORSE THAN DEATH. Cautiously, Bernhard lifted his head and peered through the knothole at the maze of red brick paths below, looking for possible ways to escape.

To his dismay, he now saw that every one of the red brick walkways fed into the main red brick path and led directly to the front door of the Gingerbread House.

"All roads lead to Rome," thought Bernhard, his heart sinking; not knowing what that meant or where it came from, or even how it bore any relationship to his current dilemma. Then:

"Go directly to jail, stick a bone out, not your finger, before you die, do not collect two hundred dollars, never buy Board Walk"; and:

"Ring around the Rosies, pocket full of Posies, ashes ashes, we all fall down . . . "Dead!" he added for emphasis.

He could try making a dash for it, as the others had done. No. No, he couldn't do that. It wasn't safe. He'd never make it. And also, he couldn't seem to get himself unraveled from the tight ball he'd gotten himself into. Leaving the safety from under the table was no longer possible. He already knew from some place inside, that his limbs would refuse to obey.

It was as if time had stopped and he had been frozen in place by some destiny or event that would have to occur before it would start moving forward again. Who else but a witch would be able to do this to him? Who else but one who could cast evil spells would be able to stop time altogether and leave him in this fearful frozen state?

He seemed to be engaged in a contest. If he won, he would be able to get home in time for dinner. If he lost . . . He gulped. Howling demon dogs had huge appetites.

Then, almost before he knew what was happening, the witch had reappeared in the doorway, with something in her hands.

"HEEL!" she rasped to the Hell-Hound. The spell was broken. The Hell-Hound shed his fierceness as if it were nothing but a fur coat, and obediently stopped barking. Halting before its mistress, it eyed the "something" she was holding in her hands.

Now the witch held the "something" higher and turned in the direction of the tree house.

"Boy!" called out the witch. "BOY? I have something here for you. I am holding a plate full of warm cookies. They just came from my oven. I won't hurt you. My dog, Flower, she won't hurt you." (FLOWER? thought Bernhard. He'd never heard of a demon she-dog named Flower.)

"I promise, Boy, I will not hurt you in any way. Shaking her cookie plate slightly, as if to waft its fragrance towards him, "If you come down right now, I'll give you all the cookies you can eat. I promise on my word of honor, Boy, I'll show you a short cut how to get home. In fact I'll walk you all the way back to your house so you won't be afraid if it gets dark. My name is Alice Mahoney and I WON'T HURT YOU! I swear it! In fact, I will only protect you if you will just come down. I give you my word! I'm so afraid that you'll fall and hurt yourself, so please come down from our tree house!"

Bernhard peered more closely through the knothole. As the witch stepped closer, he could plainly see the plate of cookies in her hands. He did like cookies – although the effect on young Dohrmann was nothing like the one they were having on Flower. Her entire body was shaking as if she had been seized by a convulsion, and she was rolling over on the lawn, her back end awash in leaves and dirt as she "spilled over" into the trail by the side of the lawns, doing her "good girl" tricks like the best dog ever.

Bernhard shifted his gaze back to the witch, as if something in his memory made him think that any witch with a name like ALICE might turn out to be a good witch. There were, as he knew, good witches, like Glinda in The Wizard of Oz. As a matter of fact, young Dohrmann recalled from some fairy tale or other, that if a witch gave you her name, the person who received this secret name held immediate power over the witch. He was sure only good witches ever gave you their name. Later, when he was re-telling the story at the dinner table, Bernhard spent some time explaining his rationale to all of us, as if it were more significant than other parts of his story. We all nodded as if we were quick to grasp the concept.

Bernhard also remembered that witches who swore and gave you their word of honor, became BOUND by the Law of the Universe. Such witches could lose their power if they were untrue to their own word. This more than any other memory caused young Dohrmann to uncurl from his ball under the tree house table and begin to descend. He wanted us to understand that his choice had been made after considerable reflection on the foregoing wisdom.

It was as he was taking his last look at the Tree House domain, that he remembered his magic stick.

In fact, all the magic sticks from the scouting party were in the tree fort. Everyone in the scouting party had scampered away without any protection. Young Dohrmann was afraid that none of them had made it back home alive.

He reached back into the tree house and scooped up his

personal magic stick as if his own life depended upon it. "I'm taking insurance," he said stoutly to himself as he descended, holding on to the rope banister and trying not to listen to the haunting moans and groans of the redwoods.

Alice sat on the top porch step of the gingerbread house, her overgrown dress spilling over her like a circus big top.

Even though Bernhard wasn't sure what "insurance" really meant, he tapped the ground and all three trees carefully before he began to take the wide trail down toward Gingerbread House. He never took his eyes off Alice Mahoney, although his senses were bombarded by the smells of two thousand living roses and a plateful of chocolate chip cookies. Seeing her head bob under the enormous straw hat, Bernhard thought for a moment, if only a moment, that Alice Mahoney might be a circus clown rather than a witch. Then he remembered his father's stern condemnation, in several pointed remarks, of those who judge others only on external appearance. He decided to give the witch a chance to show her goodness. (We who were listening to the tale were given to understand that this decision had NOTHING to do with the chocolate chip cookies.)

"No, no! You awful dog. You're going to frighten the boy!"

Alice cried out with another bob of her head and a wave of her hand. Her pointed hat and long rumpled sleeves certainly did make her look like one of Lewis Carroll's characters.

"Now stop it this minute. STOP IT or no cookies for you!" Alice's pitch was so stern, young Dohrmann paused in his winding way downward to the rising aroma of fresh cookies. Upon Alice's multiple commands or by some secret spell (Bernhard wasn't quite certain which) Flower fell to the grass and ceased her commotion. Her eyes had turned woefully pathetic. The red demon fire that had been so evident from the tree house, was gone.

Standing erect, which was not "tall" (Alice Mahoney was a small, old witch) and motioning with her hands to the boy, she said softly, "Come around THIS way, young man . . .Come THIS WAY." She gestured towards the pathway that led between the islands of roses to the broader sloping main path that led to the house.

Bernhard's timid steps set a peculiar flow of thoughts into motion in his four- year-old mind. He found himself wondering what it would be like to wake up in the Gingerbread House. He found himself comparing his own room in the Dohrmann home to the fabulous small viewing window in Alice Mahoney's cottage. He felt as if a magic rabbit had led him to this real-life Wonderland Garden. With each step he took, Bernhard was becoming less and less afraid.

(At the dinner table, as Bernhard proceeded with his story, describing how he felt, Mr. Dohrmann was becoming very attentive to the story as his young prodigy displayed the courage to face his fears in an unknown fairyland of roses.)

"Sit, boy. Sit!" commanded Alice, like a grandmother speaking The Law to a grandson. "I know you're scared, so here, you eat these cookies." She held one out directly to young Dohrmann's mouth, conveniently open with astonishment.

"As many as you want. Eat! I'll get some milk . . . "and mind the dog doesn't get ANY while I'm gone!"

Turning to Flower, she scolded, "You've been a bad, bad dog and you're not getting cookies now. That's your punishment for being a rascal!" With a long huff, she rose on her short, stubby legs, snatched one of the cookies from the plate she had left on the steps just below Bernhard's feet, bit into a corner and smiled and winked at him. "They're not poison, you know!"

In the next instant, the brown-shingled cottage, with its green shutters and bright green door swallowed her up.

Bernhard could hear the sounds of a refrigerator opening, milk bottles clinking and glasses tinkling. For several seconds, he sat very still under the ever-watchful eye of Flower. Then, teased by the smell of the fresh cookies, he tasted one, then another . . . By the time Alice returned with the much-desired milk, the boy had eaten several, and Flower had become the saddest of all dogs. Those cookies were disappearing too fast, and she still hadn't even had one!

Bernhard looked first at Flower and then at the dog's mistress. "Can I give Flower a cookie?" he pleaded, offering Alice a very chocolatey smile.

"Well, I don't know." Alice shook her head, fixing the dog sternly with her magic stare. "Flower, you know better than to be such a bad, BAD dog?" You have been a very naughty dog! What do YOU think you deserve for being so very naughty? So you think you deserve even ONE cookie for being so awful today?" She paused, waiting for her answer. Alice made sure Bernhard saw the twinkle in her eye.

Flower, meanwhile, was stirring up a cloud of dust with the furious waving of her tail in reply to her master's attentions. Her head started moving first in one direction and then in another, as if it were on some form of hinge.

"OK," Alice let out a long overloud sigh, as if she had just made a huge and very important decision. "One cookie." Turning back to Bernhard as if needing to be thoroughly understood: "She is as fat as a hippo and she needs to go on a diet!" This was said very sternly with a good deal of finger-pointing to Flower. "AND, not a cookie diet either, you BAD, BAD DOG!"

Bernhard was already holding out his cookie to Flower, who was stretching an impossible length of neck and nose. Her entire body was shaking, as if a powerful current had connected to her toes and legs. Then, with the gentlest of manners, a nibble first, then a full-on grasp, the cookie was gone, followed by some finger licks and a new friendship bonding ceremony.

The dog approached the stiff, blonde-haired, blue-eyed boy who stood at attention. First, a sniff-down initiation followed by a face licking that brought smiles, followed by hand waving and laughter.

It was clear that some form of adoption had taken place. The boy had become the property of the dog. Bernhard was soon petting Flower from one end to the other and then all over again, to the great delight of animal and child. Then

Flower rolled upside down for a belly rub. Alice shook her head in a knowing way, just short of full approval. She plopped down on the porch stoop, her face wreathed in a smile, and watched the boy and dog.

After a time, Bernhard returned to the porch stair by the cookie plate, and one by one, the cookies disappeared. One for him. One for Flower. One for him. One for Flower. Alice was certain a telepathic agreement had been reached. As a milk line formed around his little boy "O" mouth, he said, "It's getting dark! If I don't get home by dinner, I'm going to get in a lot of trouble."

"I know boy, I know. We had better be on our way." And then, to the boy's astonishment, since he could not recall having mentioned such a secret thing earlier, she said quite matter-of-factly, "Get your magic stick and let's be off."

Picking up the stick and looking up at her quizzically – How did she know about it? – he followed her down a wide path away from the house. It was a path in shadow and forest which he had not walked or seen before, a path of pine needles and dried redwood bark, that led to tiny earth stairs running off into the darkest, deepest forest.

As he climbed the earth stairs and proceeded on the trail

away from Gingerbread House, Bernhard turned to take one last look at the magnificent display of roses. They looked like the brightest candy display in the whole world, he thought. Then, using his magic stick like a cane, he followed the wide square back and broad shoulders of Alice Mahoney into the lower woods.

Tiny bridges marked the point between paths, and way off below was yet another green fence gate that led to even lower trails. These eventually brought them to an old dirt road. Alice was already down to the second bridge when she said, quite as if the boy were heel and toe with her, but loud enough to carry:

"I've told you I'm Mrs. Mahoney. What's your name, boy?"

"Bernhard Dohrmann," came the instant reply.

"Ah. I knew your grandfather," she declared as she opened the gate.

In a twinkle both boy and witch were out of the fenced enclosure of the Rose Garden and proceeding into the jungle of a redwood gorge. A whine and bark from Flower left no doubt how irritated she was at being left behind. Soon the whimpering was lost in the blend of other sounds from the cool deep forest.

Eventually they came to the old dirt road. Here Alice stopped and pointed up and down.

"Mark the way, boy. Mark it well. Take a look at these marker trees, and the bend in the road. Make a picture of my stairway. Grab it all into your mind. This is the short cut, and any time you wish to return to my Rose Garden, you are welcome. Day or night. Come any time. Know the way. Make good note of it. Quick, quick, we don't have all day. You'll have to come and go on your own in the future. You're way too big to have me walk you everywhere you want to go!"

And with those words, she began walking down the old dirt road at a pace that stretched the little legs that followed her.

His head was turning this way and that, seeking out landmarks. Touching unique stones, trees and other plants, as many as he could with his magic stick, he tried to think what a "marker" was. He felt he could use his magic stick to make sure an invisible twinkle light that only he could see, would guide him back. Pure Pixie Dust. He was sure of it. He could see it being sprinkled on each item as he tapped it. Alice didn't talk much and never seemed to notice his magic ways. Now and then when she did talk, unlike most adults he had met, she said things that meant something. Things like:

"Need a boy to weed when you come back," and:

"We can play games . . .have lots of games," and:

"Like to read . . . can read stories to you . . . great stories, you will like them," and:

"Like to bake . . . brownies . . .cookies . . .pies . . ."

Alice was puffing a bit and it was clear to young Bernhard that walking such a distance was not something to which her roly-poly legs were accustomed.

Finally, as if a tarp had been rolled back from a twist in the road, the remaining sky was filled with sunset. The winding dirt road ended, and much to Bernhard's surprise, exited on Old Marin Drive right by the Piambo gate. Just up from the first stand of redwoods was the gate trail home. The Boulders came into view as they walked the few more steps to the chain link gate.

"I believe that's you, I believe that's YOU," Alice said, pointing toward the trail that led upward to The Boulders.

Keeping a firm hold on his magic stick and running past the witch, Bernhard said, "I won't tell anyone you're a witch, Mrs. Mahoney, I promise."

To which she answered . . .as if a sadness had come upon

her, "Tell your father and mother . . . tell them that Alice Mahoney says hello."

The next time he looked back, almost at The Boulders, she had vanished behind him . . . poof! just like magic.

Reality Check

〰️ As the story came to an end, Mr. Dohrmann raised up in his chair and folded his arms. He leaned forward on the large dining table and stared at his son as if he just had recited the Bible out loud, cover to cover.

"Is there MORE . . .?"

Silence. The children stared at Bernhard and then at their father.

Bernhard shook his head. "No Dad. No more."

Mr. Dohrmann cleared his throat and looking at his wife, said, "Children, your mother and I have been very careful to teach you things about nature and how we live. We live in the country. Therefore, we must have respect for the things of nature. If young children wander very far off from their home, they might get hurt."

Eight heads were nodding. Even Baby Melissa's head bobbed up and down, though she was not yet old enough to understand the meaning of her father's words.

"They might fall," continued Mr. Dohrmann. "They might

get lost. They might even be attacked by animals in the woods. We have set the limits of where the children can and cannot travel . . . and you all know the limits. We have an enormous yard for you to play in. We have the upstairs yard. We have the downstairs yard. We have The Flats at the top of the hill. We have The Boulders and the "monkey grinders" for you to play in.

"Bernhard, do you know the limits set by this family?" The stare was now so fierce, big tears were welling up in young Bernhard's eyes, and the tears started to come.

"Yes, Father," he wavered.

"Bernhard, do you know that you went outside the limits?"

"Yes, Father."

"When did you go outside the limits?"

"When I left the Boulder area, Father?"

"And why are The Boulders the off-limit point, Bernhard?"

"Because that's where you can see from the house, Father?"

"That's right, that's where your mother and I and the family can SEE. So what do you think the punishment for a mistake THIS LARGE should be?"

"I don't know, Father."

"You want to teach the other children about what happens

when you break the rules, don't you?"

"I don't know, Father."

"You know that God has rules, don't you?"

"Yes."

"You know that God has laws and what happens when you break his rules, don't you?"

(A very shaky sigh) "Yes, Dad, I know."

"Then what is the punishment that is fair for the Rule you have broken, Bernhard?"

"I don't know, Dad." The answer was very mournful now and the little head was bowed. Bernhard stared down at this hands, clasping and unclasping them. Another silence, as eight pairs of eyes fixed on their brother and waited for the next speech.

"Well Bernhard, I DO know. I do know the punishment for the Rule you have broken, so let's go through it. First, you will apologize to your mother before you go to bed. You will find a way to let her know how sorry you are for making your mother worry. She was scared something had happened to you. Do you understand?"

"Yes, Dad." Two large tears splashed out of the little boy's eyes and landed on the tablecloth.

"Second, you will get a spanking by me before you go to bed. This is because you didn't ask for permission when you broke the rule. Do you think this is unfair?"

"No, Dad." The sobs were making speech difficult now.

"Third, you will have no privileges or playmates for one week. Is that all understood?"

Small, muffled voice: "Yes, Dad."

"Then, family, let's clear the dinner table and adjourn to the living room, because tonight is Lesson Night."

Looking into the Eyes of God

The dishes evaporated, the lights were dimmed, and the family headed for the smaller of the two large living rooms. This room contained only four items of furniture: a large white grand piano, a high-back easy chair with an ornate footstool, and two side chairs that framed it on either side. The pale yellow pastel flower patterns for the three matched chairs blended harmoniously with the hardwood floors and tall recessed ceilings with their carved moldings. It was a cozy grouping and its simple graceful proportions made the room feel complete, even without the customary sofas and tables.

"Brother Al, what period of music is your favorite?"

"Ah, that's easy to answer," I replied, smiling at my friend. I knew what was in store for me next, for Alan Dohrmann was a virtuoso pianist. He had written his first concerto when he was twelve and played a piano recital in Carnegie Hall at age sixteen. "Bach – Baroque and the pre-Romantic period. That would be my first choice."

While I was elaborating on the magnificence of Bach's

"Toccata and Fugue in D Minor," my favorite work of this great composer, Mr. Dohrmann was walking over to the piano, nodding his head in rapt attention.

Twilight was fading into deep dusk and the lights from several floor lamps glowed softly against the walls as he lifted his hands over the keyboard and began to play the Bach "Toccata and Fugue in D Minor."

One by one or in clusters, the children crept into the room until all nine had arrived. As soon as they were all assembled, they formed a semicircle around the great easy chair.

Each child had a favorite blanket or pillow upon which they sat. Some dragged their blankets along the hardwood floor and others clutched pillows nearly as large as themselves. I recall Bernhard and Sally were blanket-draggers, and Susan and Melissa opted for pillow-clutching. Oblivious of the others, each of "The Nine," as the servants called them, took their accustomed places and quietly busied themselves with plumping up their pillows and readying their special nesting spot. Without uttering even a word, the children gazed at their father as he played from a place of deep ritual and understanding.

The rendition of Bach was amazing not only for its beauty

and technical mastery, but for the fact that Mr. Dohrmann played the piece from memory alone. No sheet music, just the easy virtuoso's rendering. Then he broke into his own arrangement of a medley of the ancient master's works.

As the last notes sounded with power and magic, I found myself planted on the floor amidst a half moon of small children, overcome with gratitude. This virtuoso musician had paid his guest the incomparable compliment of a private concert solely designed for my pleasure.

As the children laughed and clapped, their father picked up his pipe and moved, elfin-like, over to his large arm chair. He gestured for me to sit in the chair to his right, and Mrs. Dohrmann took the one to his left. I felt like I was sitting in a theater and the curtain was about to rise on yet another act of an amazing and magical performance. Equally amazing was the fact that this evening's "play" or series of rituals was apparently commonplace to the Dohrmann clan. They expected dialogue at the dinner table. They expected virtuoso piano performances . . . and they almost took for granted these after dinner special learning sessions that were part of the family ritual. I was mesmerized by my own easy integration into the family fold. I had the distinct feeling they had somehow adopted me, and it lit a happy glow in my soul.

Suddenly it was so quiet, one could hear the whispers of the bay trees outside in the early evening winds. Mr. Dohrmann tamped his pipe and re-lit it, then carefully placed one cube of sugar in his coffee and enjoyed a lingering sip.

Mrs. Dohrmann, assisted by Forest, the faithful Dohrmann servant, had brought in a large Italian chess table and placed it into the area between the children and the three chairs. Then Mrs. Dohrmann set a small battery-operated pen light on top of the chessboard.

As their parents sipped their coffee and the children settled down, Forest returned to the room and set two candles on the side of the board that faced Mr. Dohrmann. Then he turned out all the lights and vanished.

The chessboard gleamed in the candlelight. The squares were of the finest green Italian marble separated by white clean squares of the same stone. The marble was thick, perhaps four inches from base to top, and paws and talons of large animals and birds, sculpted in ancient pewter, served as feet at each of the four corners on the board. A border of delicately complex carvings, with figures from the Middle Ages, traveled around the entire frame that held the game board. In the flickering light, the animals and carvings seemed to breathe and come alive.

"Children," began Mr. Dohrmann, his voice resonating in the room like the tolling of a church bell, "I want you each to know how you came to be in this world. It all began a long, long time ago. Your mother and I were very much younger then. We would sit in this room, only we would be all alone. We would sit here all by ourselves, and very much like tonight, we would have our coffee, and watch the night kiss the daytime good-bye. We would talk about what we planned to do in our life together, what would happen to us when we grew old together. Most of all, we would talk about having children.

"We longed to have our children come. We would talk about you all the time. We would name you, calling each one by his very own name. We would walk around the house, into your empty rooms, and we would imagine just what it would look like when you came along to occupy them.

"It didn't take very long before you all came. Each one just as in our secret hopes. Each of you more than any of the dreams we ever could have dreamed.

"In a short time your mother and I became very, very happy because you had each decided to join us in our life.

Mr. Dohrmann took another sip of his coffee and paused. "Have you ever wondered how it was that you were born? Have you ever talked about it with your brothers and sisters? Who has?"

All hands went up around the half circle.

"And who has talked about it to their friends at school?"

More hands.

"And who thinks they really know how they were actually born?"

No hands at all.

Mr. Dohrmann sipped his coffee and looked at his wife as if he had just fallen in love that moment. She smiled back at him, a smile more radiant and brighter than the candles.

"Let me tell you . . . all about the day you were born.

"On that day, you were only a breath in the lungs of God. It was a very magical day for your mother and me, because we had been on our knees praying that each one of you would be born. We prayed and prayed for over nine long years, until each one of you arrived.

"In the morning, on the day you were born, we knew the day was special. The golden way the dawn threw back the night, like old bed sheets, brought us fully awake immediately.

"At the time that we first held you, your mother and I received a new lesson ourselves. We knew that the Lord had sucked way back into those great lungs, and had spoken a huge sound, a huge out-flowing of His breath, and when He was all done blowing, and there was no more wind or breath left inside those lungs, that all that life force had been blown into you.

"You were blown up like a tiny balloon, full with the breath of God. Your mother and I knew this because in those first moments, in the hospital, you had a glow that was left over from God's work. You had a special golden pulse, that moved in and out all around your little bodies. Here, let me show you!"

Mr. Dohrmann put down his coffee cup, pushed out of the easy chair and knelt before one of the candles in front of the chess board. He cupped his hands around the candle as if to shelter it from a sudden wind that threatened to blow it out. At once the candlelight diminished, casting a shadow across the chessboard. Then, gently, he moved his hands down and away, and the candle flashed forth once more, casting light into the room and dispelling the darkness. Now he turned to the second candle, performing the same ritual — trapping, then releasing the flickering light into the room. Back and forth he went, from one candle to the other, all the while his curved pipe tightly clenched between his teeth.

"I want you each of you to notice how the light is greatest when the light is breathing and traveling out in all directions. When the light is breathing, the light is replacing the shadows and darkness with illumination. Notice as the light is breathing how far it can travel . . . right to the walls of our world and to the edge of where our vision can take us. Do you see it?"

At once, I found myself swept into the magical world of wizardry mixed with the unbridled enthusiasm of a child. Here was an extraordinary teacher who had a gift for mixing scholarly seriousness with fun and fantasy.

With his last words, he rose and placed his hands on his back, stretching as if he were a thousand years old, and settled back down into his easy chair. The children giggled at their father's portrayal of creaking age, and he winked at them before continuing.

"Children, you, each one of you, had a light like the candle. For when your mother and I first held you in our arms, the breath of God was still fresh on you. Your light was still breathing! Your light from the breath of God was still "leaking" out of your body bag. Your light was glowing like the candlelight. Your light was traveling all over that hospital room. It was the same for each one of you.

"Your mother and I were always amazed and delighted to see the work of God in your faces. Each one of you had such strong, strong light. I can remember how the shadows would disappear when your light would shine and pulse over the hospital room. For awhile your mother and I could not even speak, because you were so close to God in that moment, you were like little angels that had come to earth. You each had such brightness and light.

"But that's not the lesson.

"The lesson is, that everyone, every person, every baby, everyone you ever will meet, or see on television or in a movie or anywhere in all your life, also had a time when they were born. Each one of them had their own time and moment when they had the "birthglow" in their lives. When the light that is the breath of God was leaking from their body bags. Then as we all grow up, we forget.

"We forget who and what we are. We forget how we are made in the image and likeness of God, until all the memory of the magic inside us is erased, for a great many people erased forever and ever." Mr. Dohrmann stared long and hard at each of his children, and I noticed with a start, even at me.

"For you see, children, you see the world, even at your young ages, through the eyes of an adult. In many, many ways you already have grown all the way up. Let me tell you how old you are when you see things.

"You see people in the way that adults see people. Adults who have forgotten all about their birth glow, when their light had the power to take away the shadows in life. You see people as tall, and as short, don't you?"

Heads nodded.

"You see people as men and as women, don't you?"

Heads nodded.

"You see people as fat and as thin, don't you?"

Heads nodded.

"You see people as pretty and as handsome and as ugly and as not pretty sometimes, don't you?"

Heads nodded.

"You see people who talk or walk funny and those that are 'normal,' don't you?"

Heads nodded.

"You see people in wheelchairs, and who are deaf or blind,

and people who are walking and who see and who hear, don't you?"

Heads nodded.

"You see people as adults see people, don't you? But do you see their zippers? Uh?"

And no heads nodded at all.

"DO YOU SEE THEIR ZIPPERS? No, of course you don't. Because then you would need to have the eyes of God and you only have the eyes of adults.

"For you see, my children," he tamped and puffed at his pipe until the embers glowed red, "God has the eyes to see what is real, while adults have eyes to see only the reflection of what is real. The reflection is not the truth!

"In God's eyes, he makes us all equal. You have heard this from when we read the Bible and study together, haven't you?"

Heads nodded.

"I want you to do an exercise."

Everyone paid very close attention, and we all participated, even Mrs. Dohrmann. "Is everyone ready?"

Heads nodded.

"I want you to stand up. I want you to stand behind your pillows and blankets in the candlelight.

erfection
"CAN" Be Had!

"Keep your hands at your sides and be calm while I tell you what to do.

"While you are standing, I have asked God to give you the sight that the Lord has. I have asked that just for a moment, in your young life, you have the eyes that God looks through.

"Does everyone want to look through the eyes of God?"

Heads nodded (mine, too).

"Then I want you, each in your own way to do the following. I want you to realize that your bodies are not the truth of who you are.

"I want you to look at each other. Carefully. Look up and down from feet to head and see if on anyone you can spot the zipper." And here the children giggled and looked at one another, up and down, until finally it was quiet again and everyone was looking back at Mr. Dohrmann.

"Anyone see a zipper?"

And everyone shook their heads . . . no.

"I thought so. You still can't see with the eyes of God when you look, even upon your own brothers and your own sisters. How much harder must it be when you look upon your friends in life, or even upon strangers, to hold the God vision in your life path – Hmmm?

59

"I want to teach you the lesson. God sees you in a special way and I want you to see as God sees. I want you all to pretend that inside you is the same birth light that you held when you were born. All that you are, and all that you will ever become is contained in the musical notes and breath of God, that IS you, and IS me and IS everyone else.

"I want you to find the light that is inside your body bags. Your body bags are born and your body bags die. But the light that is you is trapped inside, and will one day be released again. I want you to find your own zippers that hold the light inside, and I want you to UNZIP your body bags. I want you to wiggle out of your body bags and then just sit back down and float for a minute without them.

"So now, children, unzip your body bags and let them fall to the floor. Find your zippers and let them fall and then float to the floor in any way you want to."

Children are amazing little actors and actresses. With the minimum of cues they will assume the roles that are set upon them, and perform each role to virtual perfection. Somewhere along the way to total amnesia, we forget this acting skill as fully functioning adults and never again experience quite the perfection our childhood delivered. As an adult I was privileged to revisit that perfection on the evening in which the children of Alan G. Dohrmann unzipped their body bags.

Mr. Dohrmann could not hide his delight as we all wiggled in our own way. Some of us took hold of our zipper and moved it down, and then wriggled out, until the body bags were deposited on the floor. Some stepped out of them. Some brushed them off. Some separated in other ways. We all watched the way the others did theirs. It was a partnership in becoming.

As soon as each child finished, quietly they took their position on the floor and waited.

Mr. Dohrmann leaned forward in his chair. Resting his pipe in the great ashtray, he placed his elbows on his knees, reaching his hands towards the children in explanation. His eyes traveled over the group, pausing for a few moments on each of them. "Children, you are now orbs of light. I want you to close your eyes. I want you to see each of your brothers and sisters with their Birth Light. I want you to see what happens when you step outside of the body bag you have chosen to play in during this life.

"See one another as brilliant orbs of light that are flashing, in and out, breathing, in the image and likeness of God. I want you to float just above your places, each a bright ball of light, each moving in and out, each expanding and contracting, each breathing in God's Breath.

"As you sit in this glow, I want you to feel perfect. I want you to hold an inner knowing that you no longer have colds, or coughs, or get sick, or have hurts or pains of any kind.

"I want you to slowly notice that you don't have any anger. You are no longer holding hurt feelings from some word or phrase, and the idea of these hurts and pain is like a weight, like putting on a coat that you don't wish to wear.

"I want you to GLOW and feel LIGHT!

"I want you now to turn to your brothers and sisters, but only in your mind, with your eyes closed. And I want you to see an amazing sight, as you LOOK THROUGH THE EYES OF GOD.

"I want you to see that there is no big or small, there is no tall or short. There is no fat or thin, there is no boy or girl, there is no pretty or not pretty, there is only Light. Just the same stuff. Turn and see in all directions. And then see that Al Dela Rosa and your mother, and yes, your father, are just the same. The same light in the eyes of God. All around the world there are no blacks, or whites, or Chinese, or Japanese, or Europeans, or native peoples, nor are there any other points of separation in the vision of the Lord, children. The Birth Glow is all there ever is. The rest is not Light, but reflection. Reflection is not truth, children.

"For all reflection is light that has become distorted through time and perception, the limited perception of adults.

"In these few moments, just breathe. See the Birth Glow in your family. See the Birth Glow inside every eternal spirit that has come into this life. Have a deep knowing that it never matters if they can see their own light, or share a knowing of the light within them. That is important. Create a warm fire inside your own soul that signals that the only life event that matters, in all the many things that will happen to you in your life, is if you can hold the Memory of the Birth Glow in every thought, every word, every action you ever take in life. For if you think and speak and act in the light of the breath of God, then you will experience all things through the eyes of God.

"Learn the lesson that there are only two kinds of people in this world, children: the people who remember the Birth Glow, and the people who have forgotten. Try and seek out those who remember, and live your life beside THEM. For if you choose to live beside those who have forgotten, you will forever be alone, even when surrounded by many friends.

"Remember not what is different about us. Remember only that in the sight of God, there are only orbs of Light, and the Light is always the same. Remember that in this Light there is only love. Love that fills you with peace and joy as you cast your thoughts to one another. Joy that is fulfilling and perfect in the LIGHT.

"It is only when you put your body bag back on, that the weight of separation will come upon you again. The heavy burden of seeing with adult eyes, when your judgments hold truth as reflection rather than truth from the Source of all Light. Then and only then will you once again be boys and girls, big and small, old and young, thin or not so thin. Only then will the heavy weights once again, like an old fisherman's overcoat covered with lead fishing weights, be taken upon your Orb of Light.

"Do you like your Birth Light, children? Do you like your Birth Glow? Do you like seeing and feeling it once again?"

All heads nodded, including mine. I realized that somehow I had become, in this evening, one of the children. I can't explain it, but I knew it.

"I want you to know this lesson, children. I am your father, and I will always love you best when I can see you floating, flickering, with your body bags off rather than when you zip them up and carry the weight around, forgetting the power and peace that is within your soul.

"Now! Everyone stand up. I want you to carefully reach down to the floor, and I want you to pick up your individual body bags, the ones you have chosen to play in while you are going through this life. Be careful of them, children. I want you to hold them and look at them as old familiar friends, as a costume. I want you to see that you are playing a role, of all the millions of possible roles, you have chosen to play Bernhard, or Mark, or Geof, or Melissa, or Pam, or Susan. I want you to think as you hold onto your body bag, that you will play this role the very best way you know how.

"I want you to give the Lord God the best performance for a Bernhard Dohrmann that the Lord could ever receive. I want you to give the best Carol Dohrmann, the best Sally Dohrmann that the Lord God could ever receive. And I want you to learn the lesson . . .

"THAT IT IS FOR THIS PURPOSE THAT YOU NOW PUT YOUR BODY BAGS BACK ON.

"I want you to now wiggle back into your body bags and zip them up."

I can remember how it took some time for some of us to start. Most of us were not eager to put our body bags back on. All of us looked at one another one last time. I know in my case it was to fix in my mind the candles, the light and the memory of the Birth Glow from each one of the spiritual beings in the room, into the fiber of my being for eternity. As I began to step into my body bag I remember how unpleasant it was. I could almost smell things I found too opaque to inhale. I noted how heavy the body bag was. I could see each of the children struggling to lift their body bag over their shoulders. For some it was a colossal effort. Swaying this way and that and using every last bit of strength. I found half of the children had tear-trails as they began to zip them up, and was surprised how wet my own face had become. As I zipped, I remember thinking how wonderful it would be if all peoples, in all countries, could have a day, once each year, to unzip their body bags and see with the eyes of God.

Mr. Dohrmann allowed a good deal of time to pass until all of us had once again returned to our places. As I returned to my seat beside him and looked at the children, there was an indefinable feeling of power emanating from that circle of innocence, a self-awareness that had not been there before.

"Children, I want you to remember this lesson as one of the most important of all the lessons I will ever teach you. I won't always be here to teach you, my babies. I want this lesson to be as a thread the angels give to you, to stitch together the quilt of all my other lessons, so that when you remember your father's stories you will always remember to see the lesson, with the eyes of the Lord.

"Now I want you to help me with one more part of the lesson.

"I want you to take your hand, and I want you to lower your zipper on your body bag just a bit. Everyone do it to just where you want it to be."

Some of the children took theirs down to their eyes, some unzipped themselves to their chest and some, including me, took their zippers down to their waist. The candlelight flickering like a blessing on the room gave a feeling of ceremony, and accented the children's faces in colors that only rainbows could have improved upon.

Lighting his pipe again, Mr. Dohrmann continued. "Children, you recall I taught you there were only two kinds of people in all the world?"

Mr. Dohrmann had settled quite far back in his chair now. He looked up at the candle flickers on the ceiling, perhaps seeing things that were beyond our capacity to perceive.

"Oh, I know there are children that tease you. There are children that say that you're Banana-Nose Sally, or that you're Markie Darky Larky if you're afraid of the dark, or that you're Big Butt this or that, or a thousand things that hurt your feelings. Isn't that right?"

Heads nodded.

"And I know you sometimes tease back and hurt the feelings of other children, isn't that right?"

Shamefaced, the children nodded again.

"There are adults who are almost shaking as they cry out in secret pain, children, 'I am NOT a spiritual being, I am not an eternal creature of LIGHT, I am not the breath of the Lord God, I have no LIGHT to LEAK out of my BODY Bag. While I go through this life, no LIGHT must come from me or leak out and make me wrong. I must be RIGHT in this, I need to be RIGHT!' And the up pressure on the zippers grows and grows.

"They also cry out that they must seal their body bag tight up, they must keep it so tight that NO LIGHT FROM YOU or

FROM ANYONE can ever get IN, can ever reach them, can ever pierce their heart and their secret place. The upward pressure on that zipper to keep the light of others from entering, is just as strong as the pressure to keep their own light from escaping. It is this balance of fears that makes movement so difficult, because fear can only be moved by the power of love and light.

"Do you know children or adults who you think might be keeping their body bags very tight and zipped?"

Some of the heads nodded.

"Children, I want you to know that many adults grow up and they forget so completely about their Birth Glow and their connection to the God that has created them, that they become what the Teachers of Masters call 'thumb worn.'"

"We call them 'thumb worn' because they apply so much pressure upon their zipper to assure it won't slip, not even an inch, that during their lifetime they make a small mark in their thumb. You may not be able to see the mark on their thumb, but you can feel the 'thumb worn' in your heart if you examine your feelings.

"There is nothing bad or wrong about the 'thumb worn' in life, children. They are just sleepy. They have fallen asleep and no longer are awake to the bright Light that is inside their body bag. Because they live in a world of dreams, they believe it to be real when, in fact, they are only dreams. And someday, no matter how long it takes, each, when they are ready, WILL WAKE UP. For in God's perfection, he has made one dramatic and unbreakable rule:

'The eternal soul may never remain ignorant of its own true nature.'

"Think how awful it would be if you, who now have your body bags unzipped so far down, some to your eyes, some to your chest and some to your waist, were to be compelled to live only beside the 'thumb worn' in this life. How lonely would you be? How frustrated would you be? How angry might you become? How much less laughter would you laugh? How much less happy would you be? How much less fulfilled?

"Think then, how perfect God's Plan is, that you can seek out and find others who, like you, have found they DO REMEMBER the Birth Glow. Others who, like you, have taken the pressure off their zippers. Others who, like you, wish to have movement in their life. Others who have chosen a new path, a fresh way of giving glory to God. These people we call THE RUNNERS, for they run their zippers always downward.

They have the runners of their zippers in motion.

"As in the Lord's perfect plan, the runners have eyes to see, and without accident, they will always find one another. They will form friendships and marriages. They will create their own children, and they will have grandchildren and families. From the safety of their neighborhoods of Light, they can then wander out among those who are thumb worn, those who are in pain and struggle. And simply by being themselves, they can reduce the pain that others feel. Simply by being happy. Simply by being awake. Simply by BEING — just being! They will make the pressure on the thumb of the 'thumb worn' so much less. The pain will be so much less.

"So in this lesson, children, when you find those who hurt you, who cannot understand you, who make you feel ashamed or less than, or in any way under the pain of forces you do not understand yourself, just examine your feelings. You will come back many times to this lesson. Discover when you come back to this room, to this chessboard, to this candlelight, and to our story, that you obtain a KNOWING that those who hurt you are only causing pain because they are asleep. The pain is their own pain, children, and it is not of your creation.

"Do not attach yourself to their pain or to yours. Simply

focus your attention on the person you wish to be in the moment that comes NEXT. Dwell only on the future you choose to have. Keep your attention on the Birth Glow and the Love that God has for you as well as for those who are only temporarily asleep.

"Remember, you cannot wake those who are asleep. That is the work of God. Your work is to APPRECIATE the others who are AWAKE beside you as the agents of the Lord to grant peace, joy, and fulfillment to your life. Always pay attention to which way your zipper is moving.

"Up, with less light and more pain or . . . down, with greater illumination and less pain.

"You will receive many lessons in life. You will have many hardships and trials to learn from. And in all your tests in this life, there is only one real lesson you must learn. Will you move your zipper down in forgiveness and love, accepting your lesson and increasing your ILLUMINATION for the Lord, or will you move your zipper upward and add to the darkness with anger and blame, rejecting your lessons?

"You either reject or accept your lessons in life. If you want more Light to reach you, and more Light to reach from you to others, examine your reactions to any circumstance, person

Perfection
"CAN" Be Had!

or thing, and ask yourself, 'Which way will I move my zipper?'
When you know the answer, you will have learned the lesson!"

The Game of Life

Readings were part of the Dohrmann family weekly rituals. One day each week was reserved for reading the Bible together and another day was reserved for reading fairy tales. The children's favorites were The Thirteen Clocks by James Thurber, some obscure stories by Ambrose Bierce, and the Alice stories.

Tonight was for fairy tales, and already I knew I was in for a treat.

Mr. Dohrmann began. "Children, do you remember the stories of Alice and Wonderland?"

Heads nodded.

"And the stories of Alice and The Looking Glass?"

Heads nodded.

"Do any of you know anything about Lewis Carroll, who wrote the stories?"

Everyone shook their heads "no."

"Well, then, let our story begin.

"A long, long time ago, I met Mr. Lewis Carroll. He was

very old then and I was able to spend some time with him. Mr. Carroll was a professor of mathematics at a university outside London, England, children. All of his publications, with the exception of the Alice stories and a few odd poems, dwell on mathematics. Children would find most of Mr. Carroll's writings very boring." His eyes twinkled in my direction. "So, in fact, would most grown-ups!

"When Mr. Carroll was a young man, he took a fancy to the three daughters of the Dean of his Campus on Mathematics. During the warm lazy summer days, he would row the girls around a lake in back of the grand castle-like buildings, and go for long picnics in the flower-filled meadows of the English countryside.

"It was during these journeys that Mr. Carroll created the Alice stories for the girls. They would giggle and clap and demand more and more. The stories became so popular that sometimes Mr. Carroll would have a good many children sitting around while he invented his charming nonsense.

"The parents kept pestering him to write down the tales and one day he did. When he had finished only part of the first part of Wonderland, a copy of the manuscript, written in long hand, was brought before the Queen. By Royal Invitation he was asked to bring the complete works to Buckingham Palace.

"Mr. Carroll sent the Queen a cedar chest of all his mathematical works. Later he would follow them with a set of the Alice stories tied with a large red ribbon. The printing press was coming into wide use, and the Alice stories soon became the fastest-growing publication in all the world, next to the Bible.

"Mr. Carroll, who led a very simple life, never really understood his fame, and eventually gave up any association with the stories. He spent most of the remaining part of his life in establishing new ways of thinking about mathematics.

"Everything about Mr. Carroll had some hidden meaning. In his stories about Alice, and Wonderland, and The Looking Glass, you all remember the ingredients?"

Heads were nodding.

"You remember the many strange animals that Alice met in her travels from one land to another? You remember the even stranger people that ruled the various lands Alice crossed on her way to meet the Queen?"

A crescent of children, framed in candlelight, nodded to their father.

"When you become older, you will all learn, as I have already taught some of you, how to play a game called 'chess.' For you see, Alice in the Looking Glass is not just a story, but it is in fact, a game of chess. Perhaps a perfect game of chess. Each chapter and each move within the chapter, is a move of pieces on the chessboard.

"When the babies are older I will help you read Alice In The Looking Glass and we will actually play the game of chess as we read. Would you like to learn THAT lesson?

Every head was nodding.

At this time Forest brought in, on a lovely crystal tray, the chess pieces that went with the chessboard. I will never forget how they looked. The knights, hand-sculpted by Italian artists hundreds of years ago, reared high on their horses, with lances in the air. The Queen and King were more ornate then any I had ever seen. One army was covered in gold, and the other in silver.

Mr. Dohrmann took a large castle from each side, with flags waving from long-ago turrets, and placed first one, and then the other, in the hands of a child at each end of the half circle.

"See how heavy the pieces are?" Small hands grasped the

weighty little sculptures, some needing help from one of the older children.

"These chess pieces belonged to my father, and to his father, and ultimately came to America from the King's Court in Denmark. These are very special chess pieces and I want you to always remember how special they are, because they alone can move on the chessboard that stands before you."

Mr. Dohrmann lit his pipe as the children passed the chess pieces around. I would learn later that the chessboard resided in Mr. Dohrmann's private study, where the children were not allowed. They were especially not permitted to touch anything IN the study. It was a rare treat that the magic of this amazing work of art would be shared tonight with them. The candlelight touching the golden or silver pieces made a staggering display. I found myself compelled to reach over without permission, to pick up one of the knights and gently toss it up in my hands to judge the weight. I have never before or since touched any chess pieces to match these for detail of carving and balanced weight.

"Children, I want you to put the chess pieces down, and I want you to remember them. Remember that you are very much like the chess pieces. In your body bags, you are much heavier than you might otherwise seem. And I want you to remember that God, like Lewis Carroll, is a mathematician. And I want you to understand that God had his own plan, for the game of life, when he set each one of you down on the chessboard."

Mr. Dohrmann reached over to the chessboard, and picked up the small penlight Mrs. Dohrmann had earlier deposited on it. Then he replaced the penlight with a single golden pawn. The pawn he chose was set on a white square, in the middle of the chessboard.

"I want each one of you to focus your attention now, upon the white square and not the chess pawn. I want each child in this room to BE HERE NOW. I want you to pretend. I want you to pretend that you ARE the chess piece.

"I want you to pretend that the Lord had a big plan for your life. I want you to pretend that for all your years of life, everything you know right now fits inside the chessboard square your feet have landed upon. Only I want your imagination to see the chessboard square as God sees it. For inside this chessboard square are all the things you ever learned up to right now, this night.

"As the candlelight flickers this way and that, I want you

to see that the square, as God has placed it before you, is HUGE. The square is bigger than all the stars and all the planets and all the universes you will ever study. Everything you know from school is inside this square, even the things you can no longer remember. Every book you have ever seen. Every lesson you have ever learned. Every radio program. Every conversation with every friend, with every adult. Everything you ever knew or will know is now inside this chess square.

"This one chess square.

"Only it is not day time, it is dark, late, NIGHT."

And here Mr. Dohrmann came off his chair and knelt down. Holding his pipe in his right hand, he leaned over and blew out the candle to the right side of the chessboard. This left only one candle, and the chessboard was in shadow.

"Children, it is a very dark night, and you have been standing a very long time. For years you have been standing in only one place.

"God has created a chessboard that is millions of miles long in every direction. And although you do not know it, there are teachers who have learned enough, have studied and thought and prayed so intensely that they have all the information that is contained in two or even three chess squares.

"And although you do not know it, children, there are MASTERS who, with their Light, have many more squares lit up, for they know the information in all of these squares. They make their choices and decisions in this life with all the information in many more squares than you presently have lit up in your young lives.

"And when I see you, both as your father and your teacher, I find you nearly frozen on your square. In fact, I find many adults this way as well. I find them bent over. I find them fascinated and fixed inside their life, to the information they have at their feet. Most never even look up. For the entire journey they will make in their lives, they simply never look up.

"If only I could command them to look up, to look around, to witness all the wealth of choices and abundant information that the Lord has put in their way.

"But no, these multitudes, these students, sit on bended knees, locked down to only one square (Mr. Dohrmann was still kneeling while he spoke), and these who study this way are shallow. They monitor life in the pitch-black of night, and the night is so dark, they can't even see the board itself."

Mr. Dohrmann leaned to his left and in a poof! blew out the second candle. The room went from reflected children, all leaning in on their elbows to see the chessboard, to complete and total darkness. The board simply disappeared. All that could be seen were the glowing embers in a pipe bowl and nothing more. That was when Mr. Dohrmann switched on his powerful penlight. Because of the way he held it, its narrow beam made a perfect DOT at the foot of the golden pawn, inside the one white chess square.

"When I find you, there is no moon. There is no star in the sky. There is only the small flashlight each child holds, shining between tiny feet, as they scan back and forth, back and forth, all the information that exists in their entire world. All the information between their feet. They kneel and spend all their life studying life, one simple line at a time. Never do they stand and see the information in the dot all around them. Never do they see the entire chess square and all its possibilities. Never do they see or even feel the existence of all the other chess squares God has laid around them, the unlimited potential, just waiting for human discovery.

"In fact, children, I often stumble over my students and

fall, so dark is the night that I will miss them entirely in the shadows." Mr. Dohrmann was a large, Santa-like figure, and at this point he rolled over in a large "thunk" on the hardwood floor. Some ashes fell from the pipe, tiny fireflies of light in the darkness.

Thunk!

"Children, when I pick myself up," and here Mr. Dohrmann stood as high as possible on his tiptoes, as he positioned the light moving back and forth, a tiny dot in the one white square . . .

"I always watch THEM. I watch them fascinated. I watch them hypnotized by the events of their own small lives. I watch them limited. I watch them beyond salvage as they are bound, as certainly as if they were chained to the habits of their own existence.

"And I will sneak up behind them in the dark . . . when they least expect it.

At this point Mr. Dohrmann snapped out the light. We could hear a strange scraping noise, but we did not know what it could be.

When the light came back on Mr. Dohrmann had moved a huge stepladder that nearly touched the ceiling, up against the chessboard.

"Children, as I sneak up behind the new student, all too often I find them not even aware that I have come. So as not to cause any unwanted FEAR, I will gently lift them under their arms, very softly, whispering in their ears, about their bigger future, until I guide them with me, up higher than they could normally stand. Together we will journey up an enormous ladder.

"As we rise, the student keeps his dot upon the square, but becomes amazed, for as the light rises, it expands." The dot began to expand, as Mr. Dohrmann took it higher, until it slowly began to light up the entire white square of the chessboard.

"Children, I am always amazed." He climbed a few rungs of the ladder, holding his light over the chessboard, "how my students are stunned at the new information they have discovered. Information that is as old as the stars, and has been surrounding the students all the days of their lives. Yet, as if sampling air for the very first time, each student inevitably fails to learn the lesson, and begins instead to digest the information they see inside their new field of illumination, mere moments after observing it.

"They literally soak in the information they can now see. The student dwells on each new line. Each begins, in turn, to study one new line at a time, as they become numb to the new possibilities held in fresh options that lie before them.

"It takes all the strength of the teacher to raise the student from this locked-in view, and to help them even further up the ladder. Finally, after the longest time of trial and study, I arrive at the top of the ladder before the students that follow me."

Mr. Dohrmann turned off his penlight. The room became so dark, we couldn't see what was under the black cover on the shelf near the top of the ladder. We were about to find out that Mr. Dohrmann had brought in an 800 candlepower battery-operated Navy Searchlight. This may not seem like much of an item in today's world, but back in 1952, it was a highly classified research project — which made the effect even more dramatic.

Mr. Dohrmann reached up over his head, and holding his search lamp, he continued his lesson.

"I try to break the students' fascination with the information they see in their past, and re-focus their ATTENTION on the information that lies in their future.

"No children, I say to them . . . NOOO! Please look beyond where you can see . . . Look to the edges of the chess square you are in now. See the borders. See the new ideas, the new creativity, the new possibility that touches in each direction, on all sides, and flow into directions beyond where you can see.

"What if there were a brighter light?

"What if there were a light INSIDE you that was so bright you could see beyond this point? What if you had enough LIGHT —" he switched on his searchlight "—so that you could SEE the entire chess board, children?

"You could see God's chessboard with the eyes that God has to see! You could see square after square, moving ahead and off in all directions.

"You could turn and spin." The light swept the room, illuminating the walls and ceiling, and spilled over into the next room. We all turned our heads and looked at the light while Mr. Dohrmann continued teaching us.

"Children, what if you had enough light to see all this information and you could now see so many squares. Would you live richer lives? Would you make more and better choices? Would you have better tools? BUT THAT'S NOT THE

LESSON."

Mr. Dohrmann turned off the light, and the room became even darker than before.

"THIS IS THE LESSON!

"I tell all my students, no, no, no! Do not now refocus on the information you can see. Continue.

"CONTINUE.

"Look beyond what you can see!

"Consider, what if we were in a blimp rising, and rising? Taking our light higher and higher?

"What if we were in your Uncle Walt Disney's idea for a space station that could orbit the earth and we were looking back with all that information?

"What if we were in Flash Gordon's space ship heading outside our solar system, looking back with all that new perspective?

"What if we were in Dr. Einstein's magic ship that travels at the speed of light, at speeds so fast your vision flows in all directions?"

Mr. Dohrmann turned the searchlight on the ceiling and then moved it out the window. It sent a shaft of light as far as we could see, out over the hills and across San Francisco Bay.

"No, NO, students! Look UP. LOOK beyond what you can SEE.

"The lesson is . . . always, ALWAYS increase your field of illumination.

"Always, always increase your field of vision. Do this, and your life will always contain the most information.

"Do this and your life will always be about the journey to come rather than the journey that is already over. Do this and your life will illuminate others as your vision is always reaching for tomorrow . . .

"As your vision is always reaching for the stars."

Mr. Dohrmann snapped off the Navy Search Light and Forest turned on the room lights.

Mr. Dohrmann gestured to the hallways from the top of the step ladder, saying, "And now, children, say good-night to Brother Dela Rosa and run off to bed. Your mother and I will be up to tuck you in, in just a minute."

Each of the children then got up and came over to me. Rather than take my hand, they openly displayed their affection with a hug. Some said the sweetest things this evening, and each ran off to their bedrooms, gone in a wink.

By the time it was done, Mr. Dohrmann was back in his

chair, the stepladder was removed and new coffee had been served. I remember I wanted to say something, but the only thing that kept coming into my mind was "WOW!"

As part of my training, of course I had read the works of many prominent as well as obscure philosophers and theologians, both historical and contemporary. My enjoyment of the writings of the great teachers continues to this day. It is nonetheless true that I have never since met anyone who could explain the mystery of the soul within the body, at a level easily understood by a child, as clearly and proficiently as the man who had just done so that night.

Nor have I met one who could reveal to a child the infinite love of God, the infinite possibilities we are given, as graphically as this man. The excitement of all the many choices, the love with which the lessons are given to us, and the loving insistence that we explore and learn for all of the lifetime we have been given — all of this was contained within the lesson I had just heard.

I knew that these lessons would indeed be a part of the lives of these children forever, as they would be for me. I was beginning to understand why Father Abbot had sent me to this man, and my gratitude was immense.

Mr. Dohrmann didn't ask, "What did you think?" but rather, tamping his famous pipe, "So did you learn the lesson?"

Smiling, I said that I had.

"Well then off to bed with you, and we will continue our play in the morning!"

Let Them be Runners

In the summer, Mr. Dohrmann would take the children in his Woody station wagon to a place about a half-hour away from home, on a winding road with an extraordinary view. Part of the mystery of the short journey was the increasing density of the redwood forest. As the road twisted and wound its way deeper and deeper into the forest, the shade blocked out virtually all sunlight and the ninety-degree summer afternoon temperatures would plunge to the mid-seventies. Eventually, we could come to a dark opening at the side of the road which had all the storybook mystery of a secret passageway that could only be accessed by incantation. Mr. Dohrmann would turn off the road into this opening, Camp Taylor, that today is known as California State Park.

The Woody wagon thumped and bumped into the thicket until it reached a grotto of ferns beside the streambed. A steep incline off the roadway, marked by a sliver of a trail, led to several picnic tables clustered around a barbecue pit.

Mr. Dohrmann's chase car brought up the servants and

supplies to dress the area with checkerboard tableware, wicker picnic baskets, and supplies for a feast. Soon the smell of hotdogs and hamburgers filled the air and the smoke rose in tall fingers that disappeared in the overhang of redwood boughs.

After everyone had finished, Mr. Dohrmann shuffled himself out of the picnic table bench and began moving with his elf-man walk, further down the tiny little trail. As if the Pied Piper were blowing the magical flute, the children, almost in the exact order of age, one by one, got up from their picnic tables and followed their father down the narrow trail with its dark foliage branching over the walkway on either side. Little feet made little sounds along the walkway, background to a sudden giggle or comment.

It has been more than four decades since I walked down that hidden trail in the Camp Taylor redwoods with the children. I hunger for the words to share with you what the feeling was like. The scent of the air – a mixture of earth and bark and greens, and the occasional salt water smell from the nearby sea . . .the whisper in the branches that towered above us . . . the chuckling sounds of the stream nearby . . . It was a time and place so fresh and innocent, every footfall was sacred.

As the trail twisted back and forth, it unwound like a ribbon into a circular grassy meadow, surrounded almost perfectly by tree ferns. Bernhard, who was walking ahead of me, informed me as the last bend came into view, that the "Fern Grotto" was just ahead.

The family settled itself on the flatter stones in the now familiar semicircle around their father. Behind the children was a wall of tree ferns, their wide limbs swaying gently and making a green curtain for the play that was about to begin. Mr. Dohrmann was sitting on a huge flat rock that was dead center in the tiny green meadow. The trail continued on the far side, marking this as a resting place along the way . . . a place for telling stories and gathering energy.

As I took it all in, looking up to the two-hundred-foot peaks of the redwood sentries that surrounded the place, I realized that everyone was looking at me, including Mr. Dohrmann. With my drab monk's robes, my arms enfolded in the wide sleeves, I must have cut quite a contrast to their regular routine. I returned the warm smile from Terry, the eldest, as she patted the larger stone next to her at the end of the half-circle. It was time to take my place so the story could begin. Mr. Dohrmann carefully lit his pipe, while we settled in and let the silence embrace us.

"Children," Mr. Dohrmann began all at once as if some cue had been given which only he understood, "look around you. Take some time, and look all around you."

He turned his own head from left to right and then spun around 180 degrees on the large flat stone, so that his back was facing us. We all turned around ourselves. Slowly. Looking deeply at what we were seeing. There was really nothing to see. The wood was deep. The sunlight only penetrated here and there. It was very dense. Very dark. Very ancient-looking. The massive trunks of redwoods are beyond description to those who have never seen them, and so enormous is the scale, everything in the line of sight is redefined against them. The forest is the game board itself. Everything else, life itself, composes the squares and pieces on the board.

Pipe jutting from his mouth, Mr. Dohrmann turned to face us again. He leaned forward, both elbows on his knees, his head like a lion's mane, bowing inward toward the children for emphasis.

"Children," waving his pipe toward the woods, "you have to see these forests as the place that God created to serve as the home for man. I want you to see with eyes you seldom use, so that you will see how the forest that God created really works. You may have missed this lesson. I want the lesson we learn here today to remain with you for your lifetime.

"In those years when I will not be here to sit with you and to remind you of those things you already know, I want this story of them all to bind you. I want this story to take you forward and keep you open to all the other lessons we ever have shared or will share. I want this story to be part of your foundation, as the story of the Birth Light and your body bags are part of your foundation. So I ask as our afternoon begins to fade, that you listen with all intent, as the story begins.

"In this world, there are millions and millions of people. You have seen on television how the great cities are filled with people. You have seen in books the images of China and of other far-off places. When your heads rest lightly on little pillows at night, there are places in the world just waking up. There are places with millions of people doing their lives, raising and feeding their children, and taking their children to their Camp Taylor parks, all over the world. There is never an hour or a second in which someone is not very busy "doing" their life, thinking thoughts, and feeling feelings. And this is going on, no matter what you are doing at the moment, or feeling at the time. They will never know how you feel, or how you will act. They will all proceed with their busy lives, each just as important as your own, without ever knowing you, ever understanding you, or ever coming to love you, or you them.

"We are born naked, like savage warriors before God, each without pretenses, simply standing alone and unclothed before our Maker. The great teachers know that in life, the entire journey is taken in loneliness that at times can be as painful as a raw abrasion. For, children, we are all, each in our own way, so ALONE. We never really know anyone else, never really understand anyone else, never really appreciate anyone else, unless that person takes time to slow down from their busy life and to share with us what they feel, or think, or wish to do. Even then, we may not pay attention or understand the value of the conversation.

"You will find in this life that you will give away your message, your precious secrets, with all your love and heart, to others. And you will find that they do not pay attention to you. You will find that so many you chose to share your soul with, cannot see inside and refuse to pay attention in the way that you had hoped they would.

"Some will hurt your feelings.

"Some may betray you.

"Some may show you meanness or cruelty.

"You may react and become more like them than you ever believed was possible, when you allow your feelings to rule your line of sight. When your feelings rule your line of sight, you become truly blind.

"In this life, we naked warriors are alone, by God's design, so that we can apply our FREE WILL to pick and choose our way. For in all the opportunities of life, each must be decided by the free will inside your human heart. Only you can decide.

"I cannot pick and choose for any of my children the way they will follow in their life. I cannot pick and choose to make it easier or harder. I cannot pick and choose to provide any advantage or disadvantage.

"Your brothers and sisters cannot pick and choose your way for you.

"In your choices, each will stand alone.

"If you blame others for the things that befall you in this life, you have lost your sight. You have lost your vision. For God and your soul will always know that only you have made your choices. Only you have created your possibilities, only you have selected which way to go, which way to 'be.'

"In so many ways, life is like a primordial forest. The forest is as you see here," and Mr. Dohrmann spread his hands before him. "Tall trees. Dense plants. Tiny trails leading off into the ground mist. Fallen logs. Small streams, along with a shroud of darkness.

"For the primordial forest is always in a pale of darkness. The canopy is so dense, it blocks the eternity of the LIGHT. The lungs of the earth prevent the light's penetration.

"Naked Warriors, we each, off by ourselves, each alone inside our own minds, and each wandering forever lost in the vastness of the ancient wood of the Lord. We often rest and cling to tall trees. Our fingers grope into the folds and cracks of the timeless bark, to fix our place and bind us to the earth.

"All around them, those who rest "clinging" hear the sounds of life that pass them by. The conversations. The laughter. The never-ending secrets. The noises of the Forest of Life, which frighten and bind them even more tightly to their safe positions.

"Children, those who cling, these naked warriors, are known in the Forest of Life as the MAYBES. For these few of all the millions will leave their safe little section of bark, the secure place of their clinging. Maybe once. Maybe twice.

Usually, but not always, more than once. To maybe become more. To maybe discover. To maybe become all that they imagine.

"As they carefully search the forest, attracted by the noises of life, they rarely find a brilliant illumination. These Maybes find their eyes growing larger as their hearts begin to beat faster and faster. All other sounds for them temporarily fall still, as if the forest itself had grown impossibly silent, waiting to see what the Maybes will do.

"In this moment, a preordained shift in the canopy has taken place, as the living earth breathes. And in this breath the canopy parts and a single blazing shaft of LIGHT pierces to the heart of the forest floor. A clear open pool of BRILLIANCE circles in place and stains the carpet with warmth and possibility.

"After staring with single focus on this golden circle of potential, the Maybes among us will almost always relinquish their grasp of perceived safety to journey very cautiously into the tunnel of LIGHT that has entered the whispering woods. Once illuminated, the Maybe will rise and stand tall and soak in the rays from on high. Staring full into the sky, the Maybe will reside for a time in pure joy, pure bliss, pure happiness as they stand open and empowered by the SUN.

"As an adult you will learn that all such moments last only their own time, in mysteries never made known to us, to vanish as easily as they appeared. The circle of each field of illumination will dwindle. The light will fade and the canopy will again make its shift. The great Light will disappear so totally, the Maybe will once again seek out the safety of the tree trunk by their side. To cling ever tighter. To review and reflect on the past decisions they have made.

"Many millions learn only this single lesson, to rest lower on the tree of perceived safety. As adults grow older, most of the olders in life reside on the floor of the forest. These naked warriors, men and women, will be found with their legs wrapped around the tree they have chosen. Dark with bark fragments, their fingernails dig into the soft wood of the redwood tree. They sit with their legs and feet grabbing the lower trunk of the tree. The heads of these fallen warriors are bent in, as close to the tree as possible, and their eyes remain closed and sightless. Their fear has become so great, children, that they fear the Forest of Life.

"Oh, they hear the sounds. They remain open to the whispered conversation and the shared secrets of humanity.

They only fail to participate as they once knew how. They have forgotten the earlier way of their life. No longer can they remember the way of the Maybe. Their pain has become too great.

"These naked warriors, children, are known as the FROZENS. They are frozen, to never again stand in the warmth of the sun. Never again to see the light. Never again to be one with the source of life itself. The Light!

"Why?

"The Frozen, children, have been forever damaged by the way in which the Canopy removed the LIGHT from their lives. The betrayal they remember, while forgetting their greater glory.

"The Frozen, children, only dimly remember the great moments when they lived their life in peace and joy and happiness. The time of their marriage. The time when the birth of their children occurred. The time of the perfect career. The time of the new car. The time of the new home. The time when flowers bloomed. The perfect vacation. A time when the light was shining.

"Those who grip the tree of SAFETY with fingers forever frozen into the bark, dwell upon their inner betrayals, forgetting all the joys they have also been given. Only dimly do they hear the remaining sounds from the Primordial Forest of Life that surround them in their misery.

"As you come upon these Frozens in your life path, children, and there are many, you must know you cannot help them. You cannot pry their fingers away from the bark of safety, for their need to cling is too strong."

Here, as the sunlight faded, Mr. Dohrmann rose off his large, flat, stone chair, stretched slowly and fully, and then with his unique, slow gait, went behind the children. I remember he stuck his pipe in his mouth and with fierce concentration penetrated the tree ferns, shifting branches this way and that as he peered deeply into the depth of the redwood forest. He did not speak. He did not continue with the lesson. At that moment, all of us knew in our hearts he was indeed seeing many, many Frozens, within the ancient forest. With a long, slow sigh, he let the Fern Curtain fall closed, and he returned to his teaching rock. Puffing his pipe back to life, he continued, the story drifting forth into the twilight.

"Children, these Frozens were once Maybes in their life. Once they heard the noises from the Forest of Life. Once they "let GO" as they would take first one step, then another. Once they journeyed into their life. Once they took risks. Once they made decisions. Once they left the Tree of Perceived Safety and once, maybe twice, maybe three times, they would rally enough courage and be FREE. Once, they would live, if only for some kind moments, in the pool of light from above the canopy. And children, then, and only then, during an entire lifetime, did these children of the Forest become most alive. For then and only then, children, did the Frozen live in the splendor of the SUN!

"The sun, the teacher that light always is, moves forward, leaving the Frozens behind. For these find the return of the coolness of the Forest of Life far too harsh. These find the moment when the light winks out altogether, a betrayal too mighty to bear. So great is their despair, they blame God.

"They blame God for their mistake in trusting the sun in the first place. They blame God for the loss of their relationships, their divorce, their friend who betrayed them, their career when they first heard the word "fired," their children when they found drugs. They blame God for the loss of that one child, that car accident; they blame God for their lack of success and joy and peace in this life.

"Rushing, these Maybes return from the only true

HAPPINESS they ever knew, the happiness of the memory when they stood, if only for a moment, in the fullness of the SUN while they were alive. These Maybes return to their chosen Tree of Safety and they rest, breathing so deeply in their anger and blame.

"Their legs grow weak as they sink lower and rest close to the ground to seek comfort in the soils of victimhood and martyrdom. Wiggling to sink as far as they can go into these deep, rich soils, they allow their fingers to cling to the deep ruts and scars in the ancient bark of BLAME which they will grasp for life. It will become as much a part of them as their inner nature, whose Light amnesia faithfully hides, allowing them to become Frozen.

"So hurt and so damaged by life have these children become, that they populate the Forest of life everywhere. They cling to their trees of safety as far as the eye can see. No longer can their eyes feast in the light, for their eyes now only see shadows and darkness." Mr. Dohrmann was standing and pointing across the forest and virtually shouting, before he sat once again in sad resignation with his thoughts.

During a period of quiet, Mr. Dohrmann held his head in his hands, and staring at the ground, he just shook it back

erfection
"CAN" Be Had!

and forth several times. A great sadness came over all of us. More than once our eyes wandered out into the Forest to see so clearly, the FROZENS and the MAYBES at almost every tree.

As Mr. Dohrmann raised his head to gaze at us again, his face took on an expression that contained the quality of hope. Moving his hand through the air he proclaimed, "Children, this is NOT the lesson. For YOU, children, are made in the image and likeness of God. And in this, you are most like the very source of creation in your perfect illumination.

"Your future life belongs to a simple knowing . . . a knowing that lies deep within you. You will be largely alone in this Primordial Forest of your Life, children, make no mistake about it.

"In the journey of your life, you will travel roads no one else can take for you." He looked at each individually to make sure we understood. "Your sisters cannot help you. Your brothers cannot take one step of your journey for you. Your mother cannot walk your journey for you. Your father cannot un-pry even one finger from the bark of your tree of safety, not even one small finger, children.

"Only YOU, by your own act of free WILL, can ever lift a

finger from your own chosen trees of safety.

"Your hope lies not in what we have discussed here. Not in what we have heard here. Not in what we have seen or imagined here.

"For as you walk through your own Forest of Life you will be largely naked and alone. You will pass many. Most will be Maybes or Frozens, and few will know the Forest of Life surrounds them. And in moments when you are most afraid and most fearful, when you feel most alone, and when you are sinking, your legs will feel weak. Your fingers will slide, and you will be drifting into the soft, damp soil that binds the Frozens.

"I call upon you, my children, to remember this day when you were very young, and you were very much with your family, here in Camp Taylor, in the ancient, holy precincts of this redwood forest. And I ask that you listen." Mr. Dohrmann placed his hand to his ear and leaned toward the woods, listening. "Do you hear it? Can you hear? There is the sound of movement. There is the sound of another in the forest. This sound is heard by every Maybe, in the moment when they first let go. This sound is heard by every Frozen, but long ago they have forgotten what this sound means.

"For in the Forest of life Children, there LIVES another.

"These, children, are known as the RUNNERS.

"You can hear them, for they move more swiftly then the wind.

"The RUNNERS.

"These, children, are leaping over the obstacles of life. These are running across the streams and around the giant tree trunks and dodging the barriers as they leap and playfully scream in their delight for life itself, searching with hungers born of inner knowing, for the impossible warmth of the sun.

"For the Runners, children, will pause only here and there, to spend the time they have in the glowing circle of light. For the Runners seek and never rest until they have found a fresh moment to bask in the light source of all life.

"The Runners, like everyone in the Forest, will experience the same sadness when the light begins to shrink. When the shaft of brilliance from far above the Forest Canopy begins to become smaller as the light moves to another part of the Forest, the Runners linger until the last of the illumination winks out completely and is gone. Then they bolt. They never pause or slink toward any tree of safety.

"Rather, they RUN.

"For in the vision of the mind, they see the Forest as the eagle sees the ancient cradle of all life. They see, with the eyes of creation, their Forest of Life spread itself thousands of miles in all directions. As the Runners fly off a fallen log into the trail of life, a mighty eagle lifts off from a branch behind them, and follows, sweeping with its giant wings behind the Runner, watching and searching beside this adopted traveler.

"Then, the powerful wings move and open to soar. Piercing the Forest Canopy, the Eagle rises and the mighty flyer sees the Forest Canopy is filled with illumination. Billions and billions of points of light have penetrated the Forest and shafts of brilliant light source are flowing to the floor, enough to surround every living being within.

"Of these it is only the Runner who will seek and find so many of these sacred shafts of life.

"For, children, the lesson is this: The Forest of Life is as real as any breath you ever will breathe in this life. The Forest of Life is as real as the forest you see surrounding you this evening.

"The shafts of sunlight, children, represent all that is conceivable, all the possibilities, all the rich, unlimited potential locked inside one human life.

"The Runner seeks out and finds the potentials of life. The rich marriage. The glory of children and family. Fabulous career. Adventure in vacation and exploration. Spiritual growth and purity. Truth and freedom from lies.

"The Runner experiences tragedy. Betrayal will find the Runner. For when the joy and peace of a great moment in life winks out, there is no greater sadness than the sadness held by the Runner. For the Runner alone has worked so hard to stand with an open heart.

"The Runner's vision becomes an instant hunger in the absence of light. A hunger that must be satisfied by searching for the next potential to be explored. The higher truth to be discovered. The greatest of the joys yet to be uncovered. And the Runners RUN.

"Run with all their might.

"Run with all their strength.

"Run with all their purpose.

"Run with all their being put into every footstep.

"To rest only when they next land inside the light.

"For alone in all of life, children, the RUNNERS within the Forest of Life will live their life IN THE SUN, in the warmth of the source from one moment of joy to the next.

"For the Runners have chosen.

"The Runners have made a choice.

"The Runner has no time to freeze by a tree of safety.

"For the Runner, the RUN leads only to the sun.

"I have asked in my prayers, children, that each of you find your ways in life. I have asked that when we are no longer with you, each would find peace and joy every day of your lives." His azure blue eyes sparkled like sapphires as he took his time to hold each of us in his vision.

"Now learn today's lesson, children. For when I am no longer here to teach you . . . " Leaning forward slightly, he reached into his shirt pocket and drew out a strand of nine diamonds, fondling them with his hands as if he were shuffling each gem carefully, "make my lesson today, this . . . the lesson, the MASTER LESSON to tie all your other lessons from your father into one necklace. A necklace of DIAMONDS that the Lord God has filled with all the colors of the rainbow for your spirit eye to reflect itself within. Master this one lesson, children, and you master all the lessons. You master them all."

He paused and shook his head, looking over at his wife, as if pondering a mystery known in secret between the two of them. Then he turned to us once more, gazing directly at us.

"For your mother and I do not care nearly as much as you now believe, if you have the best grades in school. Or the best anything, as you move ahead in your lives. Did you all know we cared so little?"

Heads shook, NO, DAD.

"Your mother and I do not care if you become ditch diggers or President of the United States. Your mother and I do not care if you become famous or if you are unknown by others. Your mother and I do not care if you become rich or if you are poor materially.

"Your mother and I do not care whom you may choose as your friends. We do not care if you are popular, or if you are unpopular. We do not care where you choose to live. We do not care what lifestyle you choose. We do not care if other people laugh at you or if they applaud you. We do not care how you make the choices that you make. We do not care about most of the things you may think are important to us as parents, or that YOU believe we care about." He flashed a smile at us as he looked up from the nine diamonds in his hands to his own necklace of nine diamonds from the hands of the Lord God.

"Most of all, we do not care if you please us. If you try to please us. If you do things to please us. If you act to please us. If you speak to please us. If you think that we care . . . that you PLEASE us. We do not care about THIS selfish idea, children.

"We simply don't care! It's not what you THINK.

"But mark my MASTER lesson, my sons and my daughters, because there is something that we DO care about. There is something that we care deeply about, so much in our 'core' of self, that your mother and I would give up everything we have in life to teach even ONE of our children this one magical LESSON in living LIFE fully.

"We would give up our homes.

"We would give up our cars.

"We would give up our friends.

"We would give up our jobs and things that we love.

"We would give up all these things, and so much more, for only one of you, just one child among our nine, to learn this lesson of lessons.

"Children," as he stood, he had a full command of authority in his voice and gestures, "I want you to know what your mother and your father DO WANT for their children in this life.

"Children, your parents MOST desire for you to simply live in this life as naked as life makes us all . . . as alone as life keeps us all . . . as afraid as life holds us all. We ask in our most SACRED prayers children, the prayers that mothers and fathers who worship their children as expressions of God pray at night, holding hands together, in our care for this one idea.

"Yes, your mother knows full well, that before I die, what I WISH MOST for the children of Alan G. Dohrmann, is that I may see each one of you, and IN all of you, that you have made in your life the choice . . .the single decision, the one true choice you will make between you and God. The core belief choice you make when you choose . . .

"To LIVE your LIFE in the SUN!

"I ask that you embrace your precious life and that you each choose to RUN.

"I ask that you each hear the footfalls of your brothers and sisters.

"That none of you cling to a tree of safety even for a moment in your life.

"That not one of you live your life as a MAYBE.

"That not one of my children would stop and sit and become

a Frozen . . . not even ONE . . .

"And that you EACH . . . EACH ONE OF YOU," and here he stood to his full height and gestured toward the last of the fading orange fireball in the sky, "CHOSE to live your life in the LIGHT.

"That you live as you were born to live your life, my children. For you were each born as "RUNNERS!

"Your mother and I have only seen you as RUNNERS . . . never anything but RUNNERS.

"And we ask that when faced with all your choices in life . . .

"Choices we can't make for you, or stand beside you when you choose . . .

"That before all the great choices in your life, you will pause, and return in your mind to this magic grotto. And once again you will FEEL the tall, ancient wisdom of these primordial redwood forests, and you will be still, my children, and you will listen, first to the sounds of the forest, before you make your decisions . . . and that you will fail to CHOOSE in life from the advice of the Maybes or the advice of a spirit that lies Frozen in these woods of life.

"And that you CHOOSE to take ALL your advice, advice you apply when you CHOOSE in your life, ONLY from your

FELLOW RUNNERS.

"For they WILL understand YOU.

"For they will be your company." And here, with great gestures, he exclaimed, "Now . . .RUN, my Children.

"RUN . . . whenever you make your choices.

"RUN . . . and help your family to RUN beside you.

"RUN . . .for the fulfillment of the Lord God.

"RUN . . .for your life of achievement and happiness.

"RUN . . .until the last of your breath is gone . . .

"As you make your choice, my precious angels, to . . .

"Live your life . . .in the SUN!

"Now run back to our campground with your mother, and Brother Dela Rosa will be RUNNING right behind you, but remember to listen as you run, to hear if we all can hear the sound of the OTHER Runners who RUN beside us, in God's Forest of Life!!!!! "NOW RUN!!!"

And we all did.

The Hero's Burden...
The Three Bricks

⫸ It was late August and I had just arrived for another visit with the Dohrmanns. When I entered the Lesson Room, the family had already assembled. Mr. Dohrmann was finishing his evening pipe, and the children, dressed in their customary nightclothes were sitting in their traditional semicircle around their father's easy chair.

As was the ritual, Mr. Dohrmann's house staff had placed the half-moon of candles around himself and the children. The lights and formation produced the effect of a formal stage that separated it from the rest of the room. Father and children were the touring company, the actors for the evening's performance.

Tonight the circle was broken near Mr. Dohrmann's footstool by the placement of three knapsacks. One was red, one was silver and the third was pure, bright gold.

"Children," Mr. Dohrmann placed his pipe on the large, ornate ashtray which covered the surface of the small stand by his side and leaned forward, his elbows on his knees, to stare at them, "do you know what is in these knapsacks?"

Heads shaking "no."

"Would you like to know?"

Heads nodding "yes."

"Well, you can't know. At least not yet. First I want you to wear each one of these knapsacks tonight. I want you FEEL as you wear the first knapsack, one at a time. Then each will again take your places as you are now.

"So come up and try on the first knapsack, starting with you, baby Missy!" He held the knapsack to help her put it over her tiny baby shoulders.

And they came, first one, then the next. Each tried on the first, red knapsack. Each carried the first knapsack one full circle around the outside of the flickering candle markers. Some went directly. Most modeled and feigned mock expressions of elegance to their brothers or sisters as if it were all some form of exotic fashion show.

When they were done, Mr. Dohrmann asked each of them, starting again with Missy, to perform the same task with the second, silver knapsack.

Missy had great trouble putting on the silver knapsack.

No fashion show this time! It was heavy, and as soon as she reached the other side of the room, she was more than ready to take it off. Mr. Dohrmann just smiled and nodded to her brother, sitting next to her, to pick up the knapsack and repeat the performance. Not as much fun this time. Everyone could see that it was a struggle to wear the second, silver knapsack.

When they were done, Mr. Dohrmann said that it was now time to put on the third pure gold-colored knapsack.

Alas, no matter how hard little Missy tried, she could not even lift this gold knapsack off the floor! Mr. Dohrmann suggested that she wear it right where it lay. This didn't work either, since Missy could struggle into the knapsack and virtually lie upon it, but she could not lift it up onto her back from that position, either. Feeling a little foolish, she toddled her way back to her place inside the circle of candles.

Her stronger brother had no better luck. In fact, none of the children could lift the gold knapsack from the floor.

When the last child had finished trying, Mr. Dohrmann leaned back in his giant easy chair, his hands folded in his lap, and looked at each of his nine children.

"What have we learned so far, children?"

"We learned that one knapsack is too heavy to lift."

"We learned that you can't move the gold knapsack."

"We learned the silver knapsack is too heavy to carry around very long." And so it went.

Finally, after a long pause and nod of his head that indicated he was not pleased with the answers, their father leaned forward in his chair and began to open the first, red knapsack.

Carefully Mr. Dohrmann unzipped the red knapsack that had been so easy to wear while going around the circle of candles. Each child had had no problem carrying it. Each had clowned around, almost dancing, while they wore the red knapsack.

Reaching deep inside, Mr. Dohrmann lifted out and removed a large red brick. He placed the brick in the circle of candles, then sat back and looked at it. Nine pairs of eyes examined the ordinary-looking red brick, looking for their father's secret of just what was so special about it. Some leaned on their elbows, chins propped up on tight little fists, looking at the brick, as the light from the candles danced upon their mystified faces. No clues; nothing special about that brick that they could see. After several moments had passed, Mr. Dohrmann began to speak again.

"Children," Mr. Dohrmann said at length, "I saw you each put on a little fashion show when you wore the red knapsack that held this single Red Brick. You danced around our circle of lights having quite a time of it. You performed for your brothers and sisters. You were "light" and you were happy when you wore the red knapsack which held the bright red brick you now see before you." He gestured to the brick standing on end, inside the circle of flickering lights.

"Do you know why you found it so pleasant to wear the red knapsack, children?"

Heads shaking "no" from all the children.

"You found it so pleasing, children, because you will wear this knapsack all your adult lives. You will never take it off. You will never set it down. Every waking moment you will take this knapsack and you will tie it on your back. For, of all the knapsacks you will carry in your life, my children, this one is most FAMILIAR to you.

"For the Red Knapsack, children, contains one of the bricks of pure human nature.

"The red brick of human nature is the brick of *POPULARITY AND ACCEPTANCE.*

"Human beings love to be popular. Human beings love to

be accepted. The red brick is light. It is easy to carry. When you wear the Red Brick Knapsack, children, you can dance and play and spin all around your friends. You can show off to your brothers and sisters. There is no weight to the effort. For the effort of seeking our Popularity and Acceptance comes naturally to each of us as human beings. Everyone snickers and thinks you're funny and important when you are playing with the Red Brick of human nature. You were winning acceptance and popularity as you each walked around our circle of light.

"And I want you to remember how it FEELS to be popular and accepted. It FEELS good doesn't it, my children?

Heads nodded.

"Next, can any of you tell me the lesson of the silver knapsack?" Once again he sat back in his large armchair in silence, arms folded, waiting.

No response. The children didn't have a clue.

All eyes watched as his hands disappeared like spiders into the Silver knapsack.

Out came a small bar of pure silver, the mint stamp sharply impressed on its surface. As he placed the silver bar into the circle of lights, the tiny tongues of fire jumped and licked at it.

"Children, take a close look at God's bar of silver. I noticed none of you wanted to wear God's silver knapsack. It was more difficult for you to carry this bar of human nature. Each of you had trouble getting the silver knapsack onto your backs. I also noticed you did not want to keep it on your shoulders. You couldn't wait to get this knapsack off. I could tell that you wished you had the red brick knapsack back on, since it was far easier to lift and carry than this heavy silver knapsack.

"For, children, the lesson of the silver bar is that the silver bar is the weight of *YOUR HONOR and of TRUTH, yet another quality of the potential within your human nature!* The silver bar is much more difficult to shoulder because it carries all the weight of the first bar, the red brick of popularity and acceptance. But it also carries the full measure of its own value, the weight of honor and of truth.

"Honor and truth are qualities in human nature that are far more demanding than the easy burden of Popularity and Acceptance." All eyes were fixed on the two bars. The flickering lights danced on them like fairies.

"For, children," Mr. Dohrmann was very stern and sincere, "it costs something to HONOR another human being. It costs something to carry TRUTH in your words and your deeds as you move forward in the path of your life. And the weight of silver is far heavier if you choose to HONOR every other human being that you come across in your life. In the end, children, you will always be far more popular and far more accepted in life if you choose to meet every other human being with your honor and your truth fixed firmly on your shoulders. Notice that it is the silver brick that SHINES. Do you see it? The silver brick, children, is SHINING for the Lord God!

"You can FEEL the SHINE of TRUTH and HONOR!"

And we all felt it!

"Now remember how the silver Bar of HONOR and of TRUTH felt this night.

"And when you grow up, never forget how the badges of HONOR and TRUTH will FEEL in your life, when you carry them. If you ever feel a little weight when you are faced with the honorable action, or the truthful words, remember this night. Remember your home. Remember the silver BAR inside a circle of light — and remember your father's words!"

Mr. Dohrmann leaned back in his chair. "And so what did we learn from this point in the lesson?"

All the children agreed they had learned that the BEST way is not always the lightest and easiest way.

"Very good, although," he smiled broadly, " . . . that is not the lesson." It took much longer to unzip and remove what was inside the third gold-colored knapsack. With a nod, Mr. Dohrmann indicated to Forest that he would need assistance.

As they finally pulled it forth and stepped away, in the circle of light we could see they had set down a very large bar of pure gold. The light that danced off this item was spectacular and filled the entire circle with golden sparkles that flowed over the other two bricks. The bar of gold seemed to glow with its own light. It was spectacular.

Mr. Dohrmann settled into his chair. "Children, you may all recall that none of you could lift the knapsack of gold. Not even when two or three of you tried together to do it. Why is that, do you suppose?"

"It's too heavy, Dad."

"The answer, children, is that the bar of gold was made by GOD to hold a weight so vast, it is beyond the strength of children to lift. Yet the bar of gold is also a quality of the human spirit. But what is this weight you may ask?"

His eyes traveled around the circle of faces. "The weight of the Golden Bar, children, is the weight that God has reserved for the HERO. Oh, not the hero you see on television — the person who draws the fastest gun. Or the person who wins all the medals in sports competitions.

"We are talking about the Hero inside each one of us, the Hero who CHOOSES, the Hero who wears all the bars at once. For this hero carries the full weight of popularity and acceptance, as well as the full weight of truth and honor — while also carrying the huge added weight of the HERO's bar of gold. And you may ask what is this weight of the Hero that contains each of the other qualities in full and complete measure?

"The answer, children, is that the HERO is a person who has learned the lesson of sacrifice. First, the Hero will sacrifice in little ways. The hero may give up the need to be RIGHT in front of another. And never will they tell a soul that they have done this deed. Such is the way of heroes.

"A hero will stand up for those who stand beside them, not when it is simply RIGHT to do so, but also when it is inconvenient and costly to stand by a friendship or a mate or a child. A hero will sacrifice whatever it may cost to do the RIGHT thing, even if it is unpopular. The hero will sacrifice popularity and acceptance in favor of the TRUTH, children. Such is the way of the hero in life.

"Heroes will lay down their lives, will sacrifice their own precious life, to protect the life of another human being. A hero will carry the full weight of God's true power in the choice they make to lay down the things of this life, so that another may keep those very same things.

"This is the way of the HERO, my children, and I want you to learn the way of the Bar of Gold. Come, each of you and see how it FEELS to be a Hero."

And we all did. I can remember as I touched this bar I thought, this is, after all, only a bar of metal. But because of the words of this magical man, it radiated a richness beyond its simple monetary worth. A wealth of the spirit seemed to hover around this inanimate object. It was as if, in the home of a true alchemist, the gold itself was transmuted into the dimension of spirit and power. Our fingers captured the reflection and turned in the candlelight. He let us take our time, to have as much of the feeling of the Golden Bar as we required. Some took more than one turn. It was smooth and warmed a part of the soul, holding a magic power to bind us together.

That night, we shared something that words cannot impart, for it was at a level too profound to be expressed.

"The lesson, children, is THIS," began Mr. Dohrmann, "I want my children to learn that when you grow up and you choose which knapsack you will wear in your life, by far the most difficult and challenging will be the knapsack containing the bar of God's gold. But this, my babies, is what I wish for you to choose when you grow up. In fact, I dream of you all choosing God's Bar of Gold, as soon as you are old enough to lift the gold knapsack onto your backs.

"And yes, you will be less mobile. You will not be as free as you may have been with the red brick of simple popularity and acceptance. For when you wear God's Bar of Gold, children, the knapsack of the HERO's qualities, you, my children, will become much more rooted in your life. No longer will you need to run here and there in fear of your own popularity. No longer will you have to banter around with your lighter knapsack, hoping for acceptance, always in fear of losing either one of those two elusive qualities.

"The hero is afraid too, but heroes choose COURAGE that overcomes their fear, as they make their stand in life — a stand that always FEELS like Truth and Honor to everyone who is a witness.

"The HERO, children, is HONORED by all, for the truth

that they alone display, for the TRUTH of the HERO is forever fixed, immobile, eternal. The truth of the HERO is made in the image and likeness of God.

"And so are you.

"And when you were born, your mother and I only saw in you the golden shining of the HERO. In each of you," and he pointed in turn to each of them, "you and you and you. You were all born HEROES, my children. We brought home babies with the flickering golden light of HEROES in their tiny eyes. A shining that remains in their eyes to this day.

"For in this lesson you are learning that as you grow up, you will always hold the magic of the golden knapsack inside you. Adults can only free themselves, one life at a time, to behave in a heroic manner, my children, if they themselves CARRY the bricks from within their own knapsacks.

"And adults can miss being the hero by stopping in life to remove one or more of God's great bricks from within the knapsacks they were born with. It has always been a matter of free will and choice, what each one of us will choose to carry, my children. The choice is always ours. For we were BORN TO CHOOSE!

"Have you DONE THIS? Have any of you removed even

one brick from your knapsack already?

"Have you done this terrible thing?

"Have you removed the brick of truth and honor from your knapsack?

"Have you taken away the weight that GOD has placed upon you, the HERO's weight from your birth-ride into this life?

"For you see, children, when you choose to wear the knapsack of GOLD, the HERO's Knapsack, then I can do — and only then can I do — what I am made to do as your father.

"I can," and here he gazed intently at each child " ... LOVE YOU with all my heart and all my might and I can provide to you the LOVE that only HEROES know ... one from the other. For in giving you all the love that I have to offer to you, I will know ... MY HEART WILL KNOW ... that YOU, my children, are indeed my HEROES ... and you will then and only then, DESERVE it all!

"For now though, the night is tired and so are we. So run to bed ... but run as HEROES ... and then your mother and I will come and tuck you in with all our love ... the love we reserve for God's HEROES ... scamper off to bed!"

I found I wanted to "SCAMPER" too, as the children ran full speed, off to bed, HEROES one and all ...

When It Rains........

It was the winter of 1957, a cold and rainy afternoon. Almost two years had passed since my last visit to the Dohrmanns'. "Homecomings," as the Dohrmanns called them, were always special events with every detail taken care of. Forest would pick me up at the airport and drive me to the Dohrmann estate. As soon as I arrived at my guest quarters in The Apartments, the servants would deliver and unpack my traveling bags while Forest made fresh tea, my favorite blend.

On this first arrival afternoon, Forest and I sat for awhile sipping tea and catching up on the family news from my two years "away," as Forest liked to refer to it; just as he referred to Mr. Dohrmann's many travels as his "away time."

I learned that Mr. Dohrmann had been himself "away" in Japan, and had only just returned. Tonight, the family was preparing for the first "story" in almost three months. Following the evening meal, since it was so raw and cold outside, the family would gather in the Great Room instead of the usual Lesson Room. The Great Room had a huge fireplace and this was surely a good night for a blazing fire.

While I was resting and refreshing myself in The Apartments, I noted that Dr. Edward Deming and also the Dalai Lama had visited during my absence. And here was another gift, from Richard Nixon. The two years must have been filled with many adventures; I wondered about the stories I had missed while "away."

After a festive and loving family reunion around the dinner table, we all gathered in the Great Room. With rain pounding at the giant windows looking out to a fierce night sky, and a fire roaring in the huge stone fireplace, we snuggled together in the circle of light.

By now, the children had casually accepted my funny robes and clerical mystique, and their father's permission for them to call me "Brother Al" gave our relationship a cozy familiarity. Brother Al was asked to read bedtime stories. Brother Al was asked to play games until the rain stopped. Children fought over who would be permitted to sleep in The Apartments with Brother Al, the rarest of all treats.

The "off limits" Apartments was like a magical playground for the children. It was also rare, I learned from the servants, for the children to visit any of Mr. Dohrmann's guests who stayed in The Apartments. Meetings held in the Apartments equated to a global "think tank" in which the topics dealt with "visioneering," which was Mr. Dohrmann's name for The Work. It is possible that the phrase "imagineering" that Mr. Walt Disney so liberally applied in his later work, emerged after a 1951 visit to The Apartments.

It was also a privilege for the children to be permitted to sit in the Great Room. It was such a magical setting. Forest and his watchful staff kept the enormous blaze well stoked. Light flew out in crackling orange hues, which, when the embers exploded, sent virtual meteors of color across the polished hardwood floors. It was as if some super nova had suddenly gone wild. Like wee dragons, the vermilion hissers and sparklers fixed their eyes on the upper chimney as they made a mad dash for freedom.

We sat in silence for awhile, listening and watching the fire, letting it tell us its own private stories. The scent of wood smoke evoked ancient memories of tales told long ago by other master storytellers sitting around their fires in caves, teepees, snug houses, great castles on the moors, or in the desert . . .

What would be tonight's lesson? Surely, none of us could

tell from the "props" Mr. Dohrmann had collected and placed in the semi-circle of candlelight, in front of the children. THE CODE

Mr. Dohrmann had assembled a pile of what appeared to be tiny leg irons, made of a silver metal. In the center was what seemed to be a large printed document, very thick, with a shiny blue cover, bearing a single word, "CONTRACT." To the right was a large set of what looked like green gardening shears.

I was noticing that the older children had abandoned thumb-sucking or binki-holding and other quaint habits that I rather missed. Their attention was far more riveted and their replies more deeply compelling. They were, after all, growing up. I felt a shadow of what it must be to be a parent . . . the longing to keep them small and innocent, the determination to prepare them for life.

Mr. Dohrmann tapped one of his famous pipes upside down in the large crystal ashtray until the glowing embers disappeared. Then, turning his full attention to his nine children, he began to speak. "Children, tonight's lesson is about OWNERSHIP and LOVE. My first question to you is a simple one:

"Who owns YOU?"

In his usual manner, he sat back, hands folded patiently in his lap, and stoically waited for answers to come.

Little mouths twisted and bodies pulled to sitting positions. Some whispered to each other. Several got up to join the activity center in the middle, cupping hands to ears and checking to see that Dad was not listening too closely to the suggestions. When all had settled back to their semicircular configuration, much like a television game show, they all wore the same expression of triumph.

The answer was given by Terry, the oldest. "Why, you own us Dad!" Tiny heads nodded in agreement, and some smiled confidently.

"So you believe that your mother and I OWN you?" Mr. Dohrmann leaned forward to check the belief system of his nine children individually. "Is that your answer then?" He gazed intently at the children, waiting for confirmation as if testing common resolve.

Several nodded their heads and Terry repeated, "Yes, you own us, Dad. We all belong to you and to Mom."

"Well, what I want you to DO, children, is, starting with you Terry, the oldest, I want you to place the leg irons I brought here, onto your legs. I ask that the older ones help the younger ones until it is done. Let's start one at a time. Forest will help you if you need assistance."

This was not an easy assignment. Mr. Dohrmann leaned back in his chair and watched, offering no support. The task was even more challenging when the younger children discovered they could easily step out of their leg irons. The older ones had to teach them how to shuffle their feet to keep the bracelets on their tiny ankles. I can see all nine children standing in their semicircle, turned toward their father, leg irons fastened, obediently waiting for further instruction.

Without speaking, Mr. Dohrmann rose up out of the chair and approached Terry. His adult frame hulking over her, he picked up the end of the chain from her leg irons. We saw that it had a handle fastened to it, with a length of chain leading to the first leg iron.

Then, Mr. Dohrmann began to walk. At first, as he pulled the chain, the children didn't understand. With his back to them, exerting only a slight pressure on the chain, it quickly became clear that he wanted his children to follow his lead.

So it began. The little shuffle of feet. The clankety-clink of the chains dragging across the hardwood floor . . . Mr.

Dohrmann careful not to pull on the "runner" in front as the procession slowly moved forward. Mrs. Dohrmann fled from the room to hide her giggles and also to snatch up her Brownie Camera to capture a photo for the family album.

It was inevitable that a leader or follower would jerk and pull the person they were chained to, which created some friction. A little back pull upset the balance of some of the others, causing the smaller ones to almost fall down. Mr. Dohrmann circled the giant sofa and passed three times by the fire before he was done. During the second pass around the track, smiles from the experimental chain gang procession vanished as each child concentrated on the task at hand. They were learning that they had to cooperate in order to keep moving forward together. In the first pass there was a lot of pulling and jerking accompanied by — "That's not funny!" — "You jerk-head! — "Hey! Watch it!" . . . What do you think you're doing?!!"

In the second and third pass, everyone was focusing on cooperation and they had established a rhythm for moving forward together. The third loop was by far the most difficult, since Mr. Dohrmann had begun to pick up the pace. As his lead chain pulled, the children would shuffle and try to keep up. The occasional jerk on the chain of another became more frequent – and so did the exclamations.

Finally, Mr. Dohrmann came to a halt, dropped the lead chain and returned to his chair. For a time, he watched the children in silence. Facing him like a platoon ready for inspection, hands at their sides, the children waited for further instruction.

"Children, take off your leg irons, put them in front of you when you return to your lesson positions."

Hands folded in his lap, Mr. Dohrmann waited. He didn't even reach for his oversized pipe resting in the crystal ashtray by his side.

After the children had unfastened themselves, they sat in silence, waiting for further direction.

"So children, tell me. How did that FEEL when we shared our procession of LIFE?"

"It didn't feel GOOD, Dad."

"So you're telling me that the procession of life exercise DID NOT FEEL GOOD?"

All heads nodded. ....

"Let's stop to think about what we have learned so far in our studies tonight.

"First, we learned that you THINK that your mom and your dad OWN you. You feel owned. Owned by your parents? Isn't that right?"

More nods.

"So then we chained you up like we do Alexander, the dog, so he will be safe and secure. We made you safe and secure. Like we chain our bikes. Like we chain up all things we OWN. Like we protect all the possessions we have. We treated YOU just like our other possessions, because you feel OWNED, like possessions we OWN. We made everything safe and secure. You were safe with one another. You were chained to one another. You could see one another. You could FEEL one another. You could HEAR one another.

"When I jerked your chain, you jerked someone else's chain until everyone's chain was jerked. And we found we didn't like the FEELING of being jerked and pulled by the chains, did we? We learned a little how it FEELS to be owned, if only for a minute. And we didn't like it, did we? We began to FEEL a little of what it was like to be forced to do things, all nine of you together, no one an individual, all of you tied with a common chain, the chain of OWNERSHIP. For just a moment we suspended what we THINK and we were able to focus on how we FEEL about ownership. And we discovered what it is like to consider the FEELING of what happens when one HUMAN BEING tries to OWN another Human Being.

"This bad FEELING of OWNERSHIP might be the OWNERSHIP of a husband for a wife, or a parent for a child, or a boyfriend for a girlfriend, or a friend for a friend, or a brother for a sister, one human being owning another human being.

"And we learned that OWNERSHIP chains us to FEELINGS we do NOT like.

"But, of course . . .that's not the lesson! "Sitting next to the pile of chains is a legal agreement. I want you to learn that God's universal law is stronger than all the chains in the world.

"Yet how does our human law FEEL? Can you FEEL the human law of ownership? Do you think you can?"

"We don't know, Dad," came the uncertain answer.

"But do you think you can FEEL human laws of ownership?" Without waiting for a reply this time, Mr. Dohrmann continued with the lesson.

"See that shiny blue folder in the middle of our circle here?" He pointed to the envelope resting next to the pile of chains.

"That document is a bunch of agreements. What it says is that you children are all adopted. All nine of you. You're old enough to KNOW what adopted IS.

"What this document says to you is that your mom and I adopted you all when you were very, very little, and then we brought you home. This paper says we OWN you. The paper says we OWN you right now and forever. This paper says we own you in the future for as long as you will live. We don't know who your real mommy and daddy are or where they are. We just know that WE OWN YOU because of this paper."

Here Mr. Dohrmann paused and leaned back in his chair to let the children think about what he had said. He asked again, "SO HOW DOES IT FEEL, CHILDREN, TO BE OWNED?"

"It feels terrible, Dad . . ."

"Now the part about being adopted IS NOT true, my babies. You ARE our real children." It was a good thing he imparted this information, since the younger children were starting to cry, "but I want you to tell me HOW IT FEELS to be OWNED in this way."

"It doesn't FEEL GOOD, Dad."

Mr. Dohrmann continued, "And you said, after some

thought and discussion with each other, that you believed, and we have many times learned how powerful a belief IS, that your mom and your dad OWNED you. Yet each time we show up to OWN you, we find it DOESN'T FEEL good to you. Hmmm. Let's see. What have we here?"

And at this point Mr. Dohrmann reached over and picked up the large green shears and examined them as if he had never seen such an item before. "Children, these are not really scissors. It is a wire cutting tool." He bent down and asked each child to help him cut the chains that held the shackles.

Soon the shackles, no longer connected to the others, lay in front of each child. Next, Mr. Dohrmann asked the youngest children to help him to carry the legal document labeled "Contract" to the fireplace, where he instructed them to throw it into the blaze. First he showed us, however, that all the pages inside were blank. We all watched the flames consume this pretend document.

I personally felt a tremendous relief in learning that the very idea of an adoption for even one of these nine precious children had become vapor. In the process of examining how I was feeling about this, I reflected on Mr. Dohrmann's earlier words. Indeed, a belief can have a powerful effect on our "core being," and a suggestion can also be very powerful. How important it is to guard our feelings and beliefs from "unwanted intruders"!

While we were watching the fire consume the last of the book of blank pages, Forest was placing a folded wash rag with a little colored pail in front of each child. Then he placed in front of Mr. Dohrmann a thimble on a little wash cloth, a bucket, and a large waist-high barrel. After the barrel was in position, Forest and the other servants who had been helping him, removed its lid.

Now, leaning forward, his arms resting on his legs, chin cupped in his hands, Mr. Dohrmann began. "Children, we have learned that ownership is a funny concept. It's not exactly what we thought it was, this thing called OWNERSHIP.

"We have learned that anything you really, really CARE about is best left free of chains and shackles, and should have no binding agreements of any kind to control or limit the LOVE you possess. We have learned that only GOD owns that which is created, and GOD made sure that we were all set FREE from birth. We were set FREE when we were created, with FREE will. We have always been FREE and we must always BE FREE.

"Free of any chains.

"Free of any agreements.

"Free to return or withhold our love. The one true freedom.

"However, we put chains on ourselves, and we limit ourselves when we make binding agreements, that seek to grant ownership to another, to control our lives. We have learned that only when the SHEARS OF PURE LOVE go to work to set free our beliefs and our prison chains, do we begin to FEEL really FREE again. Only when we burn our limiting beliefs and self-imposed agreements with ourselves – so the transformation of such illusory beliefs of ownership is complete — do we become truly FREE to choose.

"For you see children, it will never FEEL good to you if I own you, because you believe you have the obligation of BEING owned. It will only FEEL good to you when you surrender ownership VOLUNTARILY because you FEEL the desire for such ownership as a condition of LOVE. You give your love. You surrender your SELF as you surrender your love, as a partnership to spiritual union. Union to God first. Union to family second. Union to mates and friendships next. Spiritual union is the expression of selfless love made free of any and all conditions of ownership.

"However, this is not the lesson." A broad smile flashed across his face, conveying to the children that the magic would continue.

"I have had Forest place a different-colored pail in front of each of you. Nine children, nine colors, one for each pail. I would like at this time to have you come, one at a time, each with your pail, forming a line over here at the barrel that Forest and Majer (Forest's second in command) have brought into the Great Room. Be careful you don't spill even one drop as you learn this lesson. Fill your pails carefully. Then set each pail, without spilling even one drop, on the washcloth that is laid in front of you."

Starting with the eldest, the children began to line up by the waist-high barrel. Each, with the help of their father, filled the bucket assigned to them and, with slow deliberate steps, walked back to their places. The youngers were helped by their mother or Forest, to make sure that not even a drop fell to the hardwood floors.

As the rain continued to pound on the roof— as the storm pummeled the night — the warmth of the fire formed a comforting contrast and illuminated the next part of the lesson.

"Now that you have all settled back into your places in

life, children, I want you to know what you OWN inside your pail. Each pail is a different color because each of you experience your WAY in life individually, one from the other. Each of your pails is the same SIZE, however. Exactly the same size.

"For your pail, my children, is in truth the vessel that God has given to each human soul to hold ALL their love, the special LOVE that innocent children reserve only for their mother and father. The water inside your pail is ALL your love, my children, all the love you possess for your mother and your father. The water is all the love that can fit into your vessel. Remember always that the vessel God gave you to hold all the LOVE you possess is of a different color than anyone else's.

"For even though you all have buckets that are FULL right to the top, you also have buckets that are different from one another. This is because the hue, or the color, of your love is experienced differently, one child to the next, even though your bucket is completely and absolutely full.

"Now that you know about your bucket of love, I want you, one at a time, to carefully pick up your *love bucket* with both hands, and ever so gently, one step at a time, cross over the area to my big bucket, and dump all the water back into the great bigger bucket that has been placed beside the barrel right in front of your dad and mom. Don't spill even one drop. Now, oldest to the youngest, bring your buckets of love up here . . .

"And when you DO this, when you HEAR the water flow into this bigger bucket, I want you to THINK in your mind that you are pouring all the love you have, back to your mom and dad. You are GIVING all the love you have in your hearts to your mom and dad and putting this love into their big bucket over here." He tapped the large bucket next to the waist-high barrel.

One by one, very slowly, almost reverently, each child set a ritual and pattern for how they would give back their love. It seemed that they poured their water so slowly and deliberately, it was as if they were as if trying to stall the inevitability of arriving at the last drop.

When at length they were finished, Mr. Dohrmann peered over the bucket for some time. Then he nodded in satisfaction. His smile was always infectious and made everyone feel lighter. "So what do you FEEL now about ownership? You have given away all the love you owned from the vessel that GOD gave to you. So what have you learned?"

Considerable whispering at this point . . . a debate and shifting of positions. Then the contestants of the world's greatest game show returned to their home base. The answer, delivered smugly by the Terry, the eldest: *"We learned that we all want bigger buckets!"*

At this, Mr. Dohrmann beamed as he looked knowingly at his wife. Without saying anything more, he stood up and stretched his arms high, stretched his back. Then, without uttering a word, he bent over and with his wife's help, each lifting one side, they poured out the contents of the bucket into the larger, waist-high barrel. Together, mother and father imitated the slow deliberate way the children had poured their (love) from their individual pails into this Parent Bucket. They even tapped the sides of the great bucket when they were done, to make sure they had transferred every last drop.

I will never forget the feeling or energy during this procedure. It was as if in that moment an angelic presence had entered the Great Room, and I am certain every one of us felt it and knew what was happening.

"Children," began Mr. Dohrmann, his voice breaking as the words emerged from that deep heart place where we all felt connected, "the bucket we are lifting represents all the love that your mother and I have in this world. And although, like you, we give away the ownership of this love, we are wishing, with all our hearts, with all our souls, that the Lord God had given to us a much BIGGER BUCKET. A much, much bigger VESSEL for all of our love. However, this is the only vessel we have been given.

"And as we pour this love away, children, we pour this love into the waist-high barrel of all the LOVE we hold in our hearts for our FAMILY. For the giant barrel that is waist high is the largest of our vessels, a vessel that has been given to your mother and to me, by the Lord God, to hold all of the love we are able to give. This waist-high barrel contains all the love from all of YOUR buckets, blended with all the love from our own giant bucket, into one enormous barrel of love. And, children –

His voice broke altogether, for he was crying, and so was Mrs. Dohrmann as she faced the children . . .and then I was crying, "— your mother and I pray each night that GOD will give us a bigger BARREL to hold the love we have for you. For it is far too great for the vessel we have now. Far too great... ..FAR TOO GREAT —"

Here he did a funny thing. He patted the top of the water.

Then, with his back to us all, he just stood for awhile and gazed at his wife.

When he turned back to us, he asked that the children come up one at a time to see something magical. He held each child's hand, and gently, one at a time, patted the love that had filled the barrel. I watched this procedure nine times and still I wanted to see it repeated once more. Knowingly, he called to me to come and I did.

A pat on the water in the barrel sent a tiny ripple across the top – a wave. The magic was self-evident, for the love in the barrel rested on the top of the rounded lip. We all knew that with just a bit more force, this love would pour over the top. The wave touched all surfaces on a barrel that was FULL to a point that one more drop could not be contained.

We all felt the great connection that came from TOUCHING that LOVE. It was a feeling of being full, yet longing for a LARGER vessel . . .

As I returned to my seat, Mr. Dohrmann repeated, "And, children . . . that is NOT the lesson." Picking up the tiny thimble that was set over to his right on a small white washcloth, he held it up in the firelight and examined it from all sides.

"The lesson, children, is that many in this life do not have the family you have. Some come into the world without moms or dads to love them. Some come in and have very hard times when they grow up.

"Some are adopted and find loving families. Others are not so lucky. Some are abused. Others are homeless. And it affects them, children. It affects how they carry and protect their vessels. Many, many never discover that the vessel they own is FULL!

"And for all too many, the vessel they OWN to hold all the love they have to give away in this life, is just this tiny thimble.

"For children, the one truth you can rely upon in this life, is the truth that every human spirit will indeed OWN their OWN VESSEL for LOVE. You will find, children, that when we give our love away, when we give the love that is in the barrel of our family away," and he stood up and walked over and patted the top of the barrel, "when our hearts are on fire, there is NO vessel LARGE enough to contain all the love we pour. This love will fill a lake like Lake Mead." The children had been inside the great Hoover Dam and had seen the mighty turbines that fed the city of Los Angeles with power, so they appreciated the awesome depth of Lake Mead.

"For even Lake Mead is not large enough to contain the

love of our sacred family, my children. For this love is REFILLED every time we let it flow out. Refilled from the endless source of the Colorado River, which is God's Divine Grace.

"And the more you give away, the more that lake REMAINS full. In fact, the more Love you give away, even when all your power turbines are at full heart power in LOVE, and the Love is flowing through your dam at its greatest power, so is the Lord God providing storms such as we have this very night, that brings more water the Colorado River. The water pours in with so much Divine Grace, the FLOOD GATES must be OPENED to let the LOVE FLOW through. The "Lake" becomes SOOOO FULL at such moments, when so much love is passing through, the dam or vessel could break.

"We can fill all the thimbles and all the buckets and all the barrels in all the world, and we will still remain exactly as you see this barrel," he patted the top of the water again, "FULL. For when you give away the love of this family, children, you must know . . .

"THAT GOD WILL RAIN ON YOU.

"And this rain will fill your barrel and your lake. For God's Love is the ocean, and like the ocean, children, this supply of love is always, in every way, FULL. And from the ocean comes all the rain that flows into all the rivers that flows into all the lakes, that fills all the barrels, that fills all the buckets, that fills all the thimbles . . . and all the LOVE VESSELS remain always and precisely FULL.

"As you grow up you will choose friendships. You will choose to be married and you will, God willing, have your own children, with their own pails and your own family barrels. And as you choose your companions, your partners, your mates in this life, children, ask yourself . . .

"Is this person a Thimble, a Pail, a Bucket, a Barrel, a Lake, or an Ocean?

"Ask yourself and be very careful that you KNOW the answer before you match up your own family love. For when you begin to make your choice, you will learn the lesson of ownership.

"For you are owned in life only by the love you give away ... ...and never by the love you seek to receive. And when you learn this lesson . . ." He turned over his empty bucket and tapped it. Out poured enough water to fill the thimble right to the top.

"When you learn this lesson, your vessel will be FULL.

For you will GIVE your LOVE away to EVERYONE and you will FILL every bucket and vessel you can find, without FEAR, knowing that GOD will rain on you, filling your bucket, which will forever remain FULL. Full for YOU, Full for LIFE, full for everyone IN your life.

"And you will learn that the one truth you OWN in this life is the ownership you have for the LOVE you GIVE AWAY. For the lesson IS, children . . .

". . .you ARE God's RAIN.

"Now run to the bed you OWN, and fill your hearts with LOVE . . . as you sleep, listening to the rain . . ."

Part 2

The Tall Ships

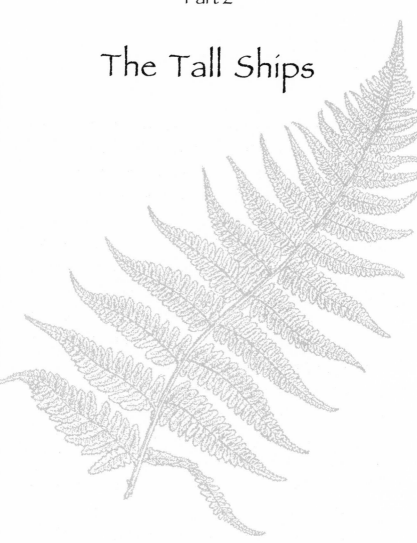

Uncle Bill

It was a hot summer day in Marin County. We were drinking Mrs. Dohrmann's famous lemonade, enjoying good conversation mixed with playful banter, when a dust cloud appeared in the lower driveway. A full-blast siren announced the approaching police car, and up thundered a specially-adapted 1950's Dodge engine with a single spinning light on top — flaring its nostrils like an angry bull. Lieutenant Bill Roberts of the San Francisco Police Department had arrived.

Bill was Mrs. Dohrmann's oldest brother and something of a hero to the children. We all laughed at Uncle Bill's grand entrance and gathered around the police car – everyone except Mother Dohrmann. Clearly, she was not very happy about her brother's reckless behavior; the driveway was right next to the children's playground. Mrs. Dohrmann explained the facts of motherhood to her older brother and set down new traffic rules for arriving and departing from the Dohrmann compound.

"Ah, Sis, you worry too much. That's what sirens are *for!*" he teased as he unfolded himself from the car to reach for the glass of lemonade she was handing him. He had already grabbed his shiny police hat off the front seat and adjusted it neatly at regulation angle. Officer Bill always wore his street blues when he came to visit the children. Basking in the reflected glory of a new television show hit, that would forever link his chosen vocation to Hollywood stardom, now he was playing the role all it was worth.

By this time "Uncle Bill" was lovingly surrounded by children who were clambering up his legs. "One, two, four, seven, NINE . . ." Uncle Bill counted. "Yep, they're all here. Not even one under the car!" And to the children's delight, he bent down and looked underneath, just for good measure. "Nope, all nine alive and well," he declared as he swooped up Melissa and Geoffrey, letting them touch the shiny badge on his uniform.

Mrs. Dohrmann cast Forest and me a mock look of hopelessness as she watched her brother shed his adulthood like an uncomfortable pair of new shoes.

I was never clear whether the fancy new San Francisco police car was really supposed to be in Marin County at that day and hour, or indeed, ever. And when Uncle Bill took all ten of us for a ride in this impressive vehicle, I believe it was quite against local police regulations – especially when he drove the car at great speed around the winding passages of the streets of Fairfax. Need I add that this particular aspect of my training was never discussed with Father Abbot, back at the monastery . . .

We all took turns pressing the siren and lights for short bursts of fun. Neighborhood pets dashed out of the way, climbing trees or barking furiously at this sudden intrusion. Other drivers tended to slow down dramatically . . . even pull over to the side.

Uncle Bill told us all about his most recent arrests, and we all were invited to see and touch his two scars from "heroic" bullet wounds, one still very much in the healing stage. The children had been taught respect for weapons and the law, and at the beginning of the excursion, Uncle Bill had wrapped his own holster and weapon in a locked car trunk.

The protruding Irish chin and humor to go with it made Uncle Bill one of the most charming individuals I'd ever met. He was a man's man who spent equal time with the ladies, making time to include everyone.

Over the next five years, to my delight, I saw Uncle Bill on several more occasions. Then one day, soon after my arrival at the Dohrmann estate for another visit, I learned from Forest that Uncle Bill had passed away that night as a result of complications from a gunshot wound. Mrs. Dohrmann was inconsolable at the loss of her older brother and best friend. Uncle Bill was so young, strong and vibrant, his absence left a huge vacuum for everyone who knew him.

Mr. Dohrmann was in Japan with his colleague, Dr. Edward Deming, when it happened, and now everyone was tense with anticipation, eagerly awaiting his arrival.

In spite of the long trip – travel at that time was far more demanding than it is today and often Mr. Dohrmann would sleep for a week after returning from the Far East – Mr. Dohrmann seemed fresh, clean-shaven and very much awake. He was wearing a clean suit and looked more like he was ready to go to Church than to bed. I learned later that Forest had delivered clean clothes at the airport, where he freshened before returning home.

Mr. Dohrmann blazed up the steep drive in the family's large new Cadillac, and accompanying his huge smile was a large bouquet of splendid white roses. As he scooped up two of the children, one on each arm, all three together held the flowers for mommy.

We had hoped all the tears would have passed by the time of his return, but upon seeing her husband, Mrs. Dohrmann almost fell into his arms. Mr. Dohrmann held his wife close and comforted her with gentle pats. Then he guided her outside as if she were made of feathers, gesturing to the rest of us to follow. Soon we were all seated in the huge new Cadillac, on our way to the country.

Sensing the somberness of their parents' mood, the children were unusually quiet. Every so often, one of them would reach over the enormous leather seats to stroke their mother's hair, pet her arm or hold her hand. As she leaned her head on her husband's shoulder, we were all wrapped in her blanket of gratitude for the comfort she was receiving from her family.

The twisting turning roadway rose higher and higher, far above the rural community of Fairfax as it existed in the early 1960's. Eventually we came to the ancient redwoods, always home to Mr. Dohrmann's soul, and host for many of his famous stories. Finally we reached the upper ridge where the steep slopes of green tumbled swiftly downward to Stinson Beach below. Here, it seemed as if there was no separation between sky and sea; both were one seamless ocean of blue. And now, the Pacific was kissing the toes of the sun which was lazily settling toward the waters on the horizon and creating a soft cloud bed for itself. We all gazed at the huge orange ball, floating without apparent movement above the thread line of the ocean's edge.

It was magic, and I think I wanted this ride to never end. With children on either side snuggled into the folds of my robes, I felt as beloved and at home as any man had a right to feel. My prayers were for Uncle Bill and Mrs. Dohrmann's grief as we wound our way down the mountainside toward the sea.

Mr. Dohrmann parked in the sand near an ancient tree, weathered and bent from many seasons. Like an elf's mushroom shelter grown immense, the circle of boughs made a cover for the car. At once, all four doors flew open and eager feet emerged.

Mr. and Mrs. Dohrmann led the way, holding hands like teenagers. Sometimes Mrs. Dohrmann would lean toward her husband and squeeze an arm or hand.

The tiny sand trail did not permit everyone to remain together and it was not long before we were making our way in single file between giant dunes. We could still hear the ocean, but it was now hidden from view. Shrubs and scrub oak dotted the sandy valleys of our walk.

I was struck with surprise at the nearness of the ocean as we walked through a break in the dunes and found ourselves at the sea's edge. No matter how often I visit it, I am always overwhelmed by the sheer immensity and staggering beauty of the sea.

No one had spoken a word until now. To say the lack of noise was unusual was to minimize the sobriety of this journey. Nine wildly active, alert, curious, playful children had made the long drive in total silence.

The ribbon of our trail disappeared into the wide expanse of sand and open beach fanning out to either side of Mr. and Mrs. Dohrmann. As I caught up with them, I could see the tender sparkle in Mr. Dohmann's eyes as he exchanged glances with his wife, and the puckish almost-smile that promised possible healings to come.

As we crossed into the wet area where the ocean grabs the sand when the tides come in, our feet made less impression, but our tracks became more pronounced. The prints were clear-cut and gave the illusion they would be etched there forever.

*Perfection
"CAN" Be Had!*

As if rehearsed, we all stopped in perfect procession, holding hands and gazing out at the sea, absorbing its healing powers. No one had given a signal or command. Not even one of the children ran up to the water the way they usually did.

We were alone on the beach and since we could see for miles, the moment seemed precious, nearly sacramental. In silent prayer, united and together, everyone held the moment. The sun, a huge red ball, was only seconds from nibbling at the sea.

Forest had placed a folding director's chair on the sand, near the damp verge but a bit on the high ground behind us. It was customary that when the entire family traveled together, a servant car would follow, carrying all the items that could not fit into the family car when it was full of children. Mr. Dohrmann turned to us and walked us back to the folding director's chair, now the focal point.

Mrs. Dohrmann sank into the chair as if her body were heavily weighted. Pain was a visible presence on the beach; it hung in the twilight with no place to hide.

With only a single gesture from their father, the children spread out on either side of their mother's chair. Once seated, they turned toward the sun, watching the magnificent sunset.

Although I have traveled the world and seen many other sunsets, I am certain that none was more perfect than this one. It held a gift.

After some moments, as if there had been much preamble and discussion on the topic, Mr. Dohrmann continued. I say "continued," because his storytelling really had no beginning or ending. Each lesson was a partner to every other one. It was if he were holding in his soul a magical abacus that contained all the ingredients a spirit in this life would require, and just at the right time, with a formula he alone commanded, he would release one more bead.

It was simply that his whole life was a magical story, and at any given moment he could open the curtain and invite others in, allowing us to view the wonder of it through his eyes.

Thus, as on other occasions, Mr. Dohrmann looked up and simply continued as if we had all been interrupted only for a second or so. "Children, this is my first day home now, and I want you all to share with me the love I hold for the sea. In just a moment, children, the sun . . ." and here, Mr. Dohrmann turned his back to us, with a grand gesture as if he had purchased the setting sun for his personal theater, "this SUN, this incredible perfect red ball, is about to kiss the sea. And when he puts his lips upon the magic sea, children, he kisses the day good-bye. This kiss of good-bye sends many subtle changes flowing everywhere upon the earth."

Brow furrowed, Mr. Dohrmann turned to tamp his pipe and ponder his next words. "Subtle changes, children. The mountains that tower behind us will now become less tall. In only moments, the outlines of these mighty peaks will soften in God's twilight. The trees upon the slopes will lose their definition and contrast. As long as the sun remains hanging, the trees hold dominion, each with sharp spires and individual authority. Soon, however, after even a single kiss to the sea, each tree will begin to blend with its neighbor. Each will become first a small group and then a vast single shape of gray. The very colors of the day will begin to fade. The greens and gold and all the rainbows in our flowers, and even the contrast between mountain summit and sky, between cloud and ocean, will disappear into the new night.

"The day can be very hot and harsh, children. Things happen in the day. Most of your life is spent in the day. Think about it. At night we eat. We talk a little. Then we sleep. The vast amount of time we spend awake with one another is invested in the day. Most of all, all the decisions we will ever make will take place during the day, children, not during the time we spend asleep in life.

"Eventually the day will become so soft and so faded, each of us will sleep. Can you imagine how it would be if we never slept, children? Can you imagine if we could never stop and reflect, or remember and look back on even one day, because the day itself never, ever ended? Isn't it perfect . . ." He waved to the red orb hang-gliding in the sky ". . . how God has engineered it so the Sun would kiss each day good-bye, and each kiss is just for us, children? Always just for us."

His eyes grew misty as he talked on. "It is this kiss that lets us know that this day is coming to an end. Each day when you see a sunset, children, I want you to stop and pause a moment. I want to you to embrace how IMPORTANT one day of time, each day of time is in the flow of your human life. Your day. This one day. Every day.

"There never comes another like it, you know." He looked off, as if puzzled by his own statement. "This day, Bernhard, is the only day, THE ONLY DAY, on this exact date at this precious time, that you will ever have, to share your hopes and dreams. For in an instant it winks out and is gone!

"And some day in the future, some day in the year 2005 on May 2nd, in the sunset, when I am no longer here to teach you such things, I want you to realize that never again will Bernhard Dohrmann, or Terry, or Pam, ever know, ever see again, a May 2nd in 2005, and such a sunset again. For the ONLY individual day you were given with that particular number, is the day that will then be passing. So, pause in your life and remember to watch God's special marker for creation, that which God calls "a day" as each sunset kisses the day good-bye.

"Mark each day. Pause and remember the worth and value. Replay each memory. Hold them as fragile truths in your life and then forever let them go.

"Twilight time is a time of wonder, children. I want you to witness the WONDER of Twilight. I want you to hold a regard for TWILIGHT. I want you to embrace, if only for a moment, the importance of marking each and every day with a spot of WONDER.

"Wonder for God who made your day.

"Wonder for all the choices and decisions you made this day.

"Wonder for all the other spiritual beings who came into

your life on this wonderful day.

"And in some way, become like the SUN as you find your own way, your own WONDERFUL way to kiss each day good bye.

"It takes so little time. It means so much if you learn to hold a spot of wonder for God's special day . . .

". . . But, children . . . this is not the lesson . . . For today's lesson is one of tall ships. Now, children, can you see how the sun is resting? The sun is tired now after his full day of labor. God has granted permission for the sun, His brilliant motor of fire and life, to rest. To lie down and sleep. For the sun, my children, lies in his very special bed made up of the horizon." And here, Mr. Dohrmann made a grand sweeping gesture as if he could contain the entire vista of the horizon before us, with the cauldron now just tipping a path of gold into the water, leading to the spot before us on the shore.

"God made the sun so that he is tucked in each and every night, like your mother and I tuck you children into your safe warm beds. Only God personally tucks in the sun, each and every night like the good parent, using the covers of the eternal sea. See! The sun *is* sinking, isn't he? He *is* diving into the sea on the far horizon . . . isn't he? It seems he is about to be tucked in for one more night of well-deserved rest."

We all felt like we wanted the sun to be rewarded for the warmth and life he shared with the planet Earth and with all of us. Mr. Dohrmann had a way of making you feel something while he told his stories. This feeling was like an electrical charge that ran though each of us. Now, the feeling was building to critical mass as eighteen eyes witnessed the blazing glory of this huge red sphere. Moment by moment, they watched it sink lower and lower, until only half of the "magic" was visible above the distant waves.

Standing on his tiptoes, Mr. Dohrmann shaded his eyes with his hand and looked far off across the sea. As he turned back to us, he exclaimed excitedly, "THERE! Do you see it?"

Pointing. "No, there!" Slightly adjusting his pointing finger, "NO! Over there, just a bit more. Do you see it children?"

Some had risen to stare as everyone sat higher in the sand, still looking. Nine, all facing the sea, tried to discover the mystery.

"THERE! Do you SEE it?" Mr. Dohrmann was animated. He would skip up toward the water, then virtually run back to us, pointing.

"The tall mast of a ship? A really big ship. Did you see the tall mast?"

He seemed to ask each of us individually. We all shook our heads "no" together, as we strained to see the tall-masted ship that he was obviously spotting directly in front of where we all sat in the sand, at the edge of a rapidly-drying, high tide line accented with seaweed, little shells, and bits of driftwood.

"There it is again!" he cried, "just coming up here!" Pointing, "and there!" Turning and pointing. "Dipping around the horizon, children. Do you SEE IT? For you MUST SEE, my children, that just a moment ago, just an instant ago, just a tip of a minute ago, just the snap of two fingers ago, to the old sailor's eye, that TALL SHIP was resting right here!" And he swept the ocean in front of the place where we were standing.

"Right here, directly in front of my family. Right HERE, where all of us could see this tall ship, with its many sails and personalities, catching the full breath of the winds of the day. And how you longed to visit that tall ship, my children."

He came up close now, and sat on the sand with his legs crossed, lighting his pipe as he shook his head with affection for his private memories.

Perfection
"CAN" Be Had!

"Oh, I CAN remember, children," he said, looking more at Mrs. Dohrmann than the children, "just the way you would tease your mother and me. Using almost any excuse over the years to get permission to visit that great tall, tall ship. For this tall ship, my babies, has a name. And the name of this ship has always been how you said it, when you said the words, 'Uncle Bill'!

"The tall, tall ship that I have seen this night, the ship I have just shown you, is to God, the ship known as your Uncle Bill. For the ship and Uncle Bill are one, my children. And oh, how the ship of Uncle Bill would love to carry you over all the waves of living life. To make you safe. To keep you dry. To carry you through any storm. To provide shelter and a nest for you to wage war against all the storms that life could bring. Safe and secure in the arms of the great ship, UNCLE BILL.

"This is a very tall, tall ship, this ship that God made. For like the big man, our ship is filled with impossible surprises. Did you know that each of you had your own special places on board the ship? Oh yes. You each have had your own nooks and crannies in the mind and heart of your Uncle Bill. Didn't you?" Heads nodded.

"Private places?"

Heads nodded.

"Secret places?"

Heads nodded.

"Places only you and the ship himself ever knew as you both shared such wonderful treasures on board?"

Heads nodded.

"You would always feel safe on board Uncle Bill, wouldn't you?"

Heads nodded.

"You would almost always giggle and laugh to run and play when you were on board "your Uncle Bill," wouldn't you?"

Heads nodded.

"You would find those quiet places in the riggings or down below the decks. Those secret hiding places and those fun, adventure-filled journeys in this place or that. Down this corridor or up another passageway. Always safe in the LOVE of your UNCLE BILL.

"For all these winding passageways on board led to some other new place of discovery inside the imagination of your tall ship UNCLE BILL.

"Eventually you all would giggle and play held up high in the upper wind, caught up in the RIGGING of your Uncle

Bill. Caught in the full sails and lines that supported how this tall ship would catch the breath of God and float FREE on the sea of forever.

"Taking you along for the ride of all the possibilities that your Uncle Bill could give to you."

Mrs. Dohrmann was crying softly now.

"Safe! On board your Uncle Bill. Laughing! On board your Uncle Bill. Playing! With your loving, magical, wonderful Uncle Bill. Held high and firm in the bold, strong RIGGING of your UNCLE BILL! For this rigging, this place where you spent so much time represents the arms of your Uncle Bill, as well as ALL the love that Uncle Bill could provide to you as children. From all the space below decks to all the cross bars of the highest rigging, contained all the full measure of LOVE this man could muster.

"Love that ran from his base foundations and keel boards to the very top of his main mast, your UNCLE BILL loved his children. You were his babies. You were why he sailed here in the first place.

"For children, your Uncle Bill sailed here in this life, just to be with you."

Some of the children watching their mother took her hand,

or leaned over on her, and most of the children had tears themselves as their father shared his feelings.

"And as you search for him . . ." Here, Mr. Dohrmann turned around and looked at the horizon again. Now just the fading shadow of the fiery disappearing sun remained above the sea. Mr. Dohrmann's face was brilliant in this reflection, as if painted in red by some hidden lens. "You look everywhere." He turned his head this way and that. "Don't you?"

Heads nodded.

"Looking. Hoping. Wishing. To BE with. To see again. To climb into the arms of that great, giant, strong rigging again, as you are held once more by all that LOVE that is your Uncle Bill!"

Tiny tears, nodding.

"For your hearts have become so very heavy, while I have been gone. Your hearts are like the lead sea weights seamen use . . . so heavy is your heart tonight, isn't it?"

Heads nodded.

"And some of you have become so sad, you don't know if you can ever be happy again, isn't it true?"

Heads nodded, and Mrs. Dohrmann nodded more than

once.

"SO sad. Your mother here is like a child herself today."

Mr. Dohrmann turned to hold his gaze on his one most priceless treasure and smiled upon her comfortingly.

"For your mother is looking for this ship, just like you are searching for this great tall mast. Your mother's gaze is even more compelling than that of your young eyes. For children, always know your mother had more time with this tall ship that we call Uncle Bill. Time when she was a little baby like some of you today. Time when she was a little older, just like some of you today. Time when she was in school like some of you older children here today.

"Time as adults, like your mom and dad, just like we are here today.

"TIME. So much time.

"So many memories.

"So many trips into the RIGGING that is your Uncle Bill.

"Your mother has tied her childhood and her adulthood and her so many journeys to and from so many ports with this great tall ship into a place she knows as HER LIFE.

"She has sailed through too many storms with Uncle Bill to stop looking now. She has been through so many adventures with Uncle Bill, she must find him. And through all this time and living, your mother has known the tight, tight LOVE rigging of the tall ship we call UNCLE BILL.

"And now, she feels maybe she will fail. Maybe the rigging is not so safe. For she can no longer, even when she strains her vision, SEE her tall ship still floating upon the sea of all possibilities . . . this sea of forever." He gestured to include all of the sea from side to side. "For you see, your mother feels because she can no longer see the tall mast of the ship we call UNCLE BILL, she might be stranded here upon the ocean, and actually be all ALONE when the next storm arises."

Some of the children had been crying and some hugged and held on to Mrs. Dohrmann, for she now she was crying very hard. Mr. Dohrmann paused, smoking his pipe, as if lost in thought. Then, just at the right moment, he continued. "Let's wait awhile to see if we can help your mother, perhaps we CAN see a bit of that great tall mast." He shaded his eyes and turned to look again upon the fading blaze on the horizon.

We sat for quite a long while holding and snuggling one another, gazing far out at the sea.

Finally, Mr. Dohrmann said, "No. No, children. I think it is beyond us to see it now. And soon it will be dark." He tamped his pipe on his shoe and the ash flew like Yosemite Fire Fall to the wet sand at the edge of the sea. "The sun has finished with our day." He was studying the fading light. "It will become very dark soon. The ocean will turn to black ink, an ink that reaches far beyond these waves to nowhere. Soon even your shadow will disappear into an ancient blackness. We must then rise and go home. For all creation will be blended into oneness and the time to rest will be upon us. We will use the light of the car to find our way home. The day that held the tall ship UNCLE BILL will be gone. Vanished forever. Complete.

"But tomorrow, my family will learn another lesson . . ."

And now, a very strange thing happened. I had never seen anything like it before, nor did anything ever match it since, during future years of Mr. Dohrmann's lesson telling.

Gently, he raised his hand to the horizon, and as if a signal had been given, a great star appeared. The star seemed brighter than any in the moonless sky that night. The way the star rose, is if on command from Mr. Dohrmann's soft gesture, it appeared to some to be the running light, twinkling like a lantern, from a very tall ship that was floating just off the horizon.

Quietly, Mr. Dohrmann rose. Again, he struck his pipe on his shoe several times, until the burning ashes had fallen completely to the sand. Then he took his wife's hand.

It had become very dark and it was more than a little challenging to find the ribbon path through the great dunes that led back to the car. I don't recall much of the ride home that night.

And then, to my surprise, it was still dark when the servants came to wake me. I was asked to dress without even bathing, and when I arrived at the car, the children were all waiting as if we just returned home. Everyone looked somewhat rumpled and in need of more rest.

Mr. Dohrmann did not speak to us on the drive back to the beach. He played classical music softly on the car radio. Some of the children slept.

As we returned to the spot of our vigil the night before, the indentations of our bodies were still apparent. Nothing had been disturbed in the hours of our departure. We nestled into the same positions.

Mr. Dohrmann sat in the same exact spot. We all looked out at the horizon, watching it grow lighter, and the servants brought us all fresh, cold orange juice.

We watched without talking, with blankets wrapped around us to keep out the morning chill. I remember thinking what a special woman Mrs. Dohrmann was for the trust she placed in her husband's intuitions at these times. She always acted as if the process we were living through was as normal as brushing teeth, reading stories or making a barbecue. Just a normal conclave on its way to bring a family of nine forward into the future. Normal as any habit of busing the children to school, or making lunch — or any custom of parenting. And yet we sat, alone for a thousand years this morning, on an ancient beach, watching a new-born sun rise over the mountain.

We sat in silence while we waited.

And then a golden hue came across Mr. Dohrmann's face first, for he alone sat farther out from the mountain's shadow. The first sliver of the new sun was rising over the majestic Marin County hills.

He jumped to his knees as if a signal switch had been thrown, and with one hand shading his eyes, he searched.

"SEE IT?" he exclaimed. "I can see it! Do you see it? The tall ship, mast first! Only that! Confirmation! Did you see it over there?" Pointing.

Some stood on tiptoes to look.

"Do you see it? Can't you see it?! There!" Pointing dramatically.

"And again . . . there!" Pointing, finger shaking for emphasis.

"Plain as the nose on your face! THERE IT IS!!!!! I see the rigging! Now more. There! The rigging!"

This rare man had hired a tall ship to sail just outside the horizon for this morning . . . only later would we know this.

Nine children rushed the shore. Mrs. Dohrmann hurried a bit herself. For the FEELING of actually SEEING the RIGGING break the horizon and a REAL SHIP show up just out of VIEW . . . to see the REAL SAILS . . . full of power and wind . . . FULL of LIFE . . . to see the MAST . . . to actually SEE IT!

Whispers.

"I see it!"

"I see it!"

"I see it, too!"

"Look! Over there!"

"There it is again!"

And always Mr. Dohrmann with: Do you see it?" Pointing.

As it fell back beyond our point of view, Mr. Dohrmann sat again and simply shook his head, gazing down at the sand. Then, he looked up and said, "But, children . . .that IS NOT . . . the lesson . . . Children, look behind you!" It was such an emphatic command we all stared. Mrs. Dohrmann and I were sitting arm in arm and we both turned together.

"Look behind you! Do you see the sun is waking from his sleep? To rise and play in God's playground of the SKY? See how the sun leaps to play in this first new day created just for YOU! This rare and precious new day. Like no other before or ever after. THIS NOW DAY. THIS NOW MORNING.OUR NOW MORNING.

"Do you see how sharp the hills and the trees have become again as each new finger of light tickles them to see this day as well?

"Do you see how you can now, with fresh vision, gaze out upon the sea of God's possibilities? Gaze far upon this ocean of forever? Look now and SEE! Now stand with me, children."

And soon all of us were holding hands equally spaced on either side of him, his wide-brimmed Panama hat flapping gently in the morning ocean breeze, facing the mountains . . .

and our future . . .

"See the sun rise. UP! UP! LOOK!"

Again in silence, we shared a FEELING as the miracle of the dawn washed fully over us, vibrant and alive.

"Let TODAY'S sun fill you with how different it FEELS when the new dawn sun KISSES each new day HELLO. Witness as the sun rises and lets go of the mountain to tease the valleys with his charms.

"Witness the power of the LORD who lifts the SUN as a miracle, higher into the sky.

"Witness the majesty, children, of the ONE POWER who raises up the SUN. And consider . . . As the sun rises and the distance between him and the mountain grows and grows and grows . . . how high . . . how terrifically high is the throne we call the SUN . . .

"How many miles. . .? How many units of measurement...? HOW HIGH is the PLACE where now the sun RESIDES? Think about it, children . . . HOW HIGH IS THE SUN?

". . . But children, even that is not the LESSON . . . Not for you." And here, he gestured for us to turn toward the sea. "No, not for you who have played on God's special tall ship, the tall ship we call UNCLE BILL. No, not for you who have been held and loved by this tall ship UNCLE BILL. No, not for you who will know and receive love from tall ships you will choose during the sails of your life, or other tall ships who will choose you.

"No, for you, the lesson is greater than all these words of truth up to this moment. For the lesson is this, children . . . I now ask that you close your eyes. And feeling the warmth of this great sun on your backs . . . with your eyes closed, I want you to imagine that there is One who is so great, so powerful that for this ONE LORD, the sun floats low in the sky rather than high in our mind's eye.

"For this ONE LORD turns the sun on and turns the sun off like we turn on and turn off a switch in our kitchen or bathroom or bedroom.

"For this ONE LORD simply commands, and the SUN switches on this day, my children.

" . . . And you know that for this one, this GOD, there is no TIME in which the sun is hidden. No night . . . for the LORD GOD is illuminated with perfect vision. Now open your eyes, children, and look again upon the sea. The sea that this same God has created to catch and hold the reflections of His SUN.

"Do you see how the sun rises and the rays catch along

the water as far as your vision can take you?

"Miracles . . . little mirrors that return the light in showers of spectacular colors from wave top to wave top. Do you see it?"

Heads nodded.

"You believe these truths I tell you, and yet somehow you fail to believe the greatest of ALL these truths. FOR THE LESSON IS THIS . . .

"The tall ship, my children, that you search for, has never gone. Your Uncle Bill is not . . . GONE!

"Your Uncle Bill, just as we have seen this morning," mighty gesture toward the sea, "floats just over that horizon. Just beyond your field of VIEW. Just beyond the point at which your tiny vision can hold the top of the mast for your great ship, UNCLE BILL.

"Uncle Bill has not changed or been taken away from you. Uncle Bill has simply moved forward . . . while you, my family, stayed here on the beach. I saw Uncle Bill last night just as clear and true as you saw your tall ship Uncle Bill this morning!

"Uncle Bill floats just as high and with all the power and strength you ever knew. Unchanged. Not changed at all. Uncle Bill, children, is waiting. Uncle Bill is waiting . . . for YOU.

Waiting for this family.

"Uncle Bill has you still wrapped up like tiny little Christmas presents, in the unchangeable rigging of his giant love for you.

"You, Bernhard, are held just above the mizzenmast sail. And you, Mark, are held behind the main sail. You, Geof, are being held by the main mast and you, my pretty wife, are being held higher than the crow's nest . . . caught up and entwined in the LOVE RIGGING that is this tall ship's HIGHEST POINT, this . . . UNCLE BILL.

"Held tight against all the storms you rest, the mother of this family, entwined in the strong forever shrouds and lines at this HIGHEST OF ALL POINTS, you remain ONE with a tall ship . . . known as UNCLE BILL."

Mrs. Dohrmann was standing looking at the sun, and she wasn't crying.

"For there," and here Mr. Dohrmann pointed up to the sun, which was quite elevated now, "HERE," as he pointed upward to the light, "rests a pair of eyes that carry a vision that is higher than any vision we hold down here upon this beach.

"There . . . rests a vision that can see beyond the remote horizon, and all horizons off this shore. Horizons that your frozen and stuck eyes can never see beyond.

"There, way up there, children, stands a vision that can SEE . . . see clearly . . . SEE NOW . . . IS SEEING THIS MOMENT all of what is the real UNCLE BILL.

"Can really and truly SEE your UNCLE BILL . . .

"All of your Uncle BILL.

"Just as you have always seen him.

"Nothing changed.

"Not one thing.

"Not one part of the decking.

"Not one part of the cabin.

"Not one part of the sails.

"Not one part of the love rigging.

"Not one part of ANYTHING.

"Nothing changed at all.

"Uncle BILL is alive and complete and whole.

"WAY UP THERE," pointing high.

"As Uncle Bill was yesterday, was the day before, or will be a million years from now.

"It is only YOUR VISION, your limited, frozen vision, my children, that has been changed. It is only YOUR VISION, my children, that has compelled you to remain here, with your sightless eyes, so low to the ground, frozen here, on this special beach. It is only YOUR VISION that is so limited now, so limited to its line of sight, my babies . . . that separates your seeing and feeling your Uncle Bill." He ruffled Bernhard's blonde hair more than once.

"IT IS ONLY YOUR VISION that can't see the tall mast. Only your vision that fails to see the truth. Just your limited view, nothing more.

"For your Uncle Bill floats with all his power, and all his majesty, with all his heart, with all his love, with all his spirit, with all his soul, just beyond this horizon of your sight, my children." He waved toward the sea.

"Just over there . . ." And he waved again, pointing this time.

"No, just there . . .for Uncle Bill is MOVING . . . right over THERE!" And he pinpointed the spot. At that moment I swear that once again we all saw a billowing sail and wisp of a mast spike roll beyond a wave of the great ocean.

"And one day, all too soon children, you yourself will move FORWARD, as Uncle Bill has done, within your cruise of life, and when you do, once again you will sail right by the side of your UNCLE BILL.

"For your Uncle Bill is not alone. He sails with a FLEET of TALL SHIPS that sail beside him . . . each a beacon for those who will soon move FORWARD to FOLLOW in the journey of life.

"For now . . . this early morning . . . just remember, when you THINK of your Uncle Bill, to always in ALL WAYS, adjust your FIELD OF VISION. And as you do, you will SEE with the eyes of a higher point of view.

"From this vision point you will actually SEE the tall ship we call Uncle Bill, even as we saw the tall strong mast this early dawn. So it will be every time you remember.

"And as you remember, KNOW that you, my babies, are forever entwined in the rigging of all the LOVE that is what your Uncle Bill uses to sail with."

"And that, my family, is the lesson . . . Now, let's go eat!"

And for the first time in a long while, the family was hungry once again.

Part 3

The Dohrmann Legacy

Perfection
"CAN" Be Had!

Note: This part of the book is a compilation of Brother Al's diary, the family annals and one anecdote of particular poignancy, that depicts the true essence of my father.

— B.D.

The New World

⚞ Until the mid 1970's the Name "Dohrmann" rose on the largest sign over Union Square, the full length of the now prominent brick facade of the Macy building on Geary Street. Everyone said the Dohrmann family had reinvented San Francisco. The name "Dohrmann" was a byword in the city.

The young Dohrmann — Alan Dohrmann's great-great grandfather – who, in the pre-Gold Rush era, had ventured to the New World at the age of seventeen, had no idea what was in store for him. The voyage to America had been difficult. The crew treated "the royal brat," as he was called, like everyone else. To make matters worse, toward the end of the voyage, the boy fell and broke his arm. Ship voyages were long and difficult in those days. Although the ship's carpenter set the bone with the best splints the sea would allow, the young boy was still weak and ill when he was dropped off on the wooden sidewalks of a tiny port that would one day become San Francisco. At that time it was still in the throes of changing from an Old Spanish Mission to a brash American frontier town.

Blonde, blue-eyed and quite striking, the boy did his best to remain neat and pressed, away from the horses and carriages that let the mud fly, as he strode the boardwalk looking for opportunity. This new life must have been quite a culture shock. Surely, it bore little resemblance to the royal courts of Europe.

On the second day, on the wide swath of cleared dirt known as Market Street, he found a hardware emporium with a Help Wanted sign in the window.

The boy entered the establishment, and upon striking up a conversation with the shopkeeper, learned that he was also from Germany. The shopkeeper knew of the Dohrmann family. But this didn't help; in fact, it was not exactly an advantage to be so "well connected."

Dubiously, he eyed the young man's roughly-splinted broken arm. "I'm sorry," he shook his head. "I need a lad who has the use of both arms. And someone who can, er . . . sweep the floor, empty toilets . . . Er — uh . . ." He flushed, "do things that you may not find exactly . . ." The boy understood. Such work was not fitting for "royalty." Over a cup of tea, they agreed that the position was not suitable.

As young Dohrmann turned to leave the shop, however, his eyes wandered to the stairway. At the top on a long landing was a large store of ship's brass — air covers, bell stands, braces and t-bars, winches and clenches and tools. His hand paused indecisively on the knob of the half-open door. The exit bell had already sounded.

Cocking his head and stepping inside once more, the boy closed the door behind him and turned to address the shop owner. With the assurance of one who has never suffered rejection, the young Dohrmann explained his proposition, as if it were his sole reason for crossing two oceans and journeying thousands of miles from home.

His deep blue eyes gleaming with conviction, he explained how the brass could be restored and marketed to German ship captains for their return voyages. He told the shopkeeper that he certainly had enough influence with these seamen to be able to easily set up a good business with them.

After another pot of tea and a long, slow San Francisco afternoon with occasional interruptions from customers seeking a fistful of ten-penny nails or a washtub and scrubbing board, the two discussed the terms of a new business relationship. A fifty-fifty partnership was arranged for anything the young entrepreneur could sell.

Dohrmann moved into the loft above the store, and in six weeks a number of miracles happened. First, the boy gradually regained the use of both arms. By that time all of the brass had been restored to "like new" condition. Also by that time, all of the brass had been sold. Another miracle was the way in which young Dohrmann handled the customers. His innate courtesy and well-trained intellect made them feel that he not only knew what they wanted to buy, but actually understood and sympathized with their needs as well as the difficulties of their lives. For six weeks, from morning to dusk, he clerked in the hardware store without pay. After the store was closed, he worked on his brass, and at dawn, long before the store opened, he would venture to the docks to market it.

Dohrmann kept the loft filled with newly-acquired brass and the half of the profits he was permitted to keep was immediately invested back into new supplies. He printed a business card that read simply, "EMPORIUM."

Word spread among the seamen. They were so taken with the boy's special qualities, they began to acquire everything they needed for their long sea voyages that was available in the Hardware Emporium. The store owner was pleasantly stunned at the surge in profits. Although he was not, strictly speaking, a ship's chandler, nonetheless, he could supply many of the needs of the ships' supply officers. At his new associate's urging, he began to order greater stocks of those items that served these maritime customers.

By the end of six weeks, from his own funds, Dohrmann had stocked the shelves in the store with dry goods and food staples suitable for long voyages. Soon farmers and related customers were also buying at the Emporium general Store, as it was coming to be known. Food preservation was in its infancy in those days, and those who lived on isolated farms or ranches were just as glad as the sea merchants to have a place to buy staples for long periods of time. Within six months Dohrmann was made a partner in the store, and in six years he owned it. By that time the Gold Rush had begun.

The Gold Rush

When gold was discovered in the foothills near San Francisco, the signal went out around the world nearly as quickly as it would have been delivered today by the Internet. As if a whip had cracked over the flanks of the Barbary Coast, the trumpet call of "GOLD!" brought a river of treasure seekers through the Golden Gate into the Port of San Francisco. Others came the overland route, all of them eager to grub up riches from the soil of California.

History and Hollywood have captured it all for us: the jingling harnesses and creaking wagons; gunfire; the tinkling piano and loud guffaws in the line-up of saloons where men paid for drinks with a pinch of gold dust and bartenders were hired for the size of their fingers — the larger the better . . . The wild mixes of languages and dialects; and always the smells of horse manure and leather . . .the blacksmith's clang mingling with the clatter of dishes and scoops scraping the woks in the Chinese chop-suey huts . . . Overnight, California became a crossroads and melting pot for people from all over the world with a single goal.

Young, prosperous Dohrmann had two visions of the future. First, he saw clearly that the Gold Rush was temporary, and that the foundation of wealth was not in the gold mines but in the streets and people of San Francisco. Second, although San Francisco might be built on gold, Dohrmann saw the future of the city as the railhead for the soon-to-be-completed Transcontinental Railway system that would link the West to their trading partners in the East.

By now, the wealthy young man had traveled extensively in America, and he had acquired considerable business savvy. Dohrmann believed that only the fewest of men would find their pot at the end of the golden rainbow, and with good council from friends like John Muir, Mark Twain and John Sutro, he launched into a strategy to receive gold from all of them, whether or not they achieved their dreams.

Dohrmann saw that soon the tiny creek that first answered the lure of gold would become a stream, a People Stream that grow into a People River. Thousands of people would be flowing toward the latest News of GOLD. Towns would spring up overnight and die overnight, depending on the discoveries hundreds of feet underground. Like river beds shifting their position, the gold flow would twist and pull to this place and that by the force of its own momentum.

Where would all these people stay until they had homes of their own? There were inns and hotels, but hardly enough to accommodate the swarms of prospectors. Overnight, new accommodations sprang up in San Francisco and everywhere along the gold trail. With his unique contacts in Holland and Germany at the Royal Courts, Dohrmann developed exclusive supply lines for materials not yet manufactured in quantity in the New World: crystal glasses, table linens, flatware, vases, furniture items, and more.

With courage and at great risk, the young entrepreneur opened the Dohrmann Hotel Supply Company, a one-stop shopping center for the hospitality industry. His goal was to be the exclusive supplier to the inns and hotels of the West. With virtually no competition, the Dohrmann company burgeoned, opening up offices in Seattle, Los Angeles, Las Vegas, and wherever the hotel explosion was occurring.

At the same time, Dohrmann expanded the Emporium Store to become a retail outlet for many of the items the Dohrmann Company would sell, most of which were also suitable for home use. As immigrants moved from inn to home,

Perfection
"CAN" Be Had!

Dohrmann gave them an opportunity to acquire the familiar items they would need in their households, from his now larger and much grander Emporium. Taking ideas from the emerging concept in the East of a one-stop department store, young Dohrmann opened the San Francisco Emporiums, the first major department store outlet in the Western States.

By the time of his death, Dohrmann would preside over the largest resort-outfitting organization in the world, as well as the largest department store chain in the seventeen western states. The firm was passed on to Alan Dohrmann's father, Alpert Bernhard Charles Dohrmann, or ABC Dohrmann, the eldest son, who turned the Dohrmann success into an empire.

Alan Dohrmann (---- -1983)

▟▛ During the Great depression, Alan Dohrmann, in his teens at that time, was virtually unaware of the hardships taking place for other families in the nation. He was especially proud of his father's activities during Hitler times. ABC had his own Schindler's List and brought over many Jewish refugees, employing them in his Emporium stores.

ABC Dohrmann was seldom home. He worked long hours in building such successes as the Iiawani Hotel in Yosemite Park, and, with John Muir and the President, in securing national park status for many outstanding natural spots of beauty. ABC was also expanding his Emporium and Dohrmann operations to become global forces.

The family photo albums featured portraits with presidents and kings. Historic images with President Roosevelt, or tintypes with John Muir and Mark Twain decorated the family walls.

Alan Dohrmann and his twin brother, Jerry, were among the youngest of the twelve Dohrmann children, and the second set of twins to arrive. Alan was virtually the only child to remain "free" of the wealth and power of the family empire. The rest of the family went into the business.

Upon completing his private school education, Alan entered the officer training program of the United States Navy at Treasure Island. This allowed him to enjoy the privileges of his family, and San Francisco's social life. "The Set" included the Swig Family, owners of the Fairmont Hotels, the Magnins and the Gumps.

During the war, Alan became involved in an accelerated learning project for the United States Navy war effort. Such projects had grown popular during the World War II years, when speed was essential.

Alan's training related to teaching others to handle warships such as mine sweepers and liberty vessels. Operation "Snap Shots" taught "spotters" to mentally record briefly viewed ordinance, planes and ships, seen from island assignments in the Pacific. This program changed the future of the training industry that emerged after World War II. Operation "Jump Ship" was a six-week training program that successfully taught farmers from Kansas City who had never seen the sea, to pilot liberty ships.

Bernhard: In my training sessions in Anchorage, Alaska, as is my custom, I asked the participants to share what they had learned from the day's lessons. During this particular share session, an elderly gentleman, Bill Bacon, raised his hand to speak.

Bill had arrived at the class literally looking like a snowman; the snow was so packed onto his clothing, he had to pound it off. He was accompanied by an enormous Newfoundland purebred that looked more bear than dog. Together, the old man and dog looked like a postcard from the land of the Vikings. Bill had sat quietly during the class until this time, when I asked if anyone wanted to share.

"My Name is Bill Bacon," started the old man, limping up to the podium in his cumbersome snow boots, "and I want to give young Dohrmann a gift that I have found after almost thirty years." He handed me a large, soiled brown envelope, and stepped away from the microphone, waiting for me to open up the package before proceeding with his story.

I am not ashamed to cry – not even in public, when the occasion warrants it. On this occasion, I did not even try to hold back the tears. Bill Bacon was a three-time Academy Award-winning photographer for the Disney organization. He had brought me photographs of a film shoot on location with "Uncle" Walt Disney, Roy Senior, and others who had been part of my childhood. Each photograph, signed by Bill, had its own story.

"I first heard of about Alan Dohrmann when I was a young man, doing field work in the Pacific for the Navy," said Bill. "I, and many other sailors and soldiers had heard about the Snap Shot program, and the other advanced training programs Dohrmann was part of. Many lives were saved, and many men lived, because of the work of these programs, developed over such a short period of time."

Bill spoke eloquently, calling Alan Dohrmann a hero. "No brass band will play, celebrating his heroism. Bernhard won't talk about it, but he knows what I am saying is true, and I want you all to know it's true."

He told a wonderful story about a time when he was filming with Walt Disney on location, for a picture. Bill said that he was filming Mr. Disney because he didn't often leave the studio and come on site for a shoot.

"Suddenly, Mr. Disney said to me: 'And I want you to meet MY teacher . . .' He introduced me to your father, Alan G. Dohrmann . . .later I would reflect I was never so sorry in all my life, that I did not turn the camera around from Walt, and take Alan's picture as well. It was like that with Alan. He was always invisible, standing behind the great ones he would mentor. Bernhard, I wanted you to have the pictures, so you would always recall the day that Bill Bacon almost took your dad's picture. I have held on to these pictures for just such a time, and many times I have thought about what Mr. Disney said that day, because I thought it was so extraordinary . . . 'I want you to meet my teacher' . . . It was something!"

Alan was convinced that human beings could excel if they received the right training, particularly accelerated training. As pioneer of Super learning and related disciplines, his assignments with government and private industry took him all over the world. Accelerated learning became his passion for the remainder of his life.

He also felt that accelerated training or "Super Teaching," as he later called it, would be an agent for preventing war in the future. He believed that "only through retraining human beings could the spirit of war as a destructive force be harnessed for the spirit of cooperation and creativity."

The Dohrmann family was not overjoyed to see their young son so influenced by the war and a passion for something other than entering into the family business. ABC Dohrmann was once heard to say to friends at a San Francisco party: "Teachers, we hire them; we don't invite them into the family."

ABC Dohrmann was careful to keep up his appearances. During the war, his considerable resources became a key war effort supply line, and frequently he appeared in photographs in the *San Francisco Chronicle*, accompanied by VIP's from President Roosevelt to the Secretary of Defense.

ABC was not amused when, following the war, his young son expressed a desire to work in the "human potential" business. "Imagine, the 'human potential industry' he calls it . . . whatever THAT is! I can only hope he will gain a responsibility that puts out of his head this silly notion of teaching adults who have already completed their education. Silly notions they don't require or desire."

Alan Dohrmann would never match his siblings in business passions. He never cared for it. People, not money, were his motivation.

I was born in 1948, the third child and first son born to Alan Dohrmann. I never knew my grandfather, ABC, since he had passed away several years before. After years of bickering about how things might be best run when ABC was gone, the Dohrmann and Emporium holdings were sold and the family members each went their separate ways.

In the 1970s, Alan and his oldest sister, Edith, would hold family reunions. With the exception of one brother, the entire family would attend these events.

At the time I was born, my father had just created a program known as Marriage Encounters for the Catholic Church, of which he was a lifelong member. This program took two years to perfect. It was created originally for the young men returning from the war, to resolve what he perceived as a growing lack of skill in relationships.

Alan Dohrmann had no idea that this course, designed for a single parish church, would one day influence courses to be translated into more than twenty languages, offered by over 200 denominations in one form or another, and, by the year 2000, to be instructed to millions upon millions of couples around the world. How many families have remained intact? How many marriages have remained whole or been revitalized as a result of attending these Marriage Encounter programs? Perhaps it is this program over all the other attributes of the family, that truly represents THE EMPIRE. Can there be any better legacy than a training program that teaches people how to love and live in harmony with each other?

In addition to Marriage Encounters, Alan designed a number of other human potential programs that ultimately influenced the work now known as Mind Dynamics, Lifespring, PSI World, Total Quality Management, Sage Trainings, EST, Total Value Quality, Leadership Dynamics, Visioneering, Money & You, and many others. This body of work was principally developed for major corporations and leading human potential training companies, a task that continued throughout Alan's lifetime.

The proof of Alan Dohrmann's work lives on today in the accomplishments of those graduates of scores of training programs, still taught throughout the world; and the teachers who have knowingly or unknowingly been influenced by a charming, plump, elf-like man, that only a few ever had the privilege to know about or to meet personally.

Those "light workers" who did work directly with this Master Teacher were the leaders who pursued expanded human potential in the work place, in the family, and in our society. Like treasure seekers finding a lost chest within the hull of a Spanish galleon, many of these individuals made it their practice to personally visit Alan regularly.

Alan Dohrmann was known as the "Teachers' Teacher." He was always introduced by word of mouth; he never sought his students, nor did he ever promote his work. Each new leader was always welcomed the same way, with invitations to stay at the Dohrmann estate in the complex that was known as "The Apartments." Existing as a stand-alone living facility, it was filled with every creature comfort for extended visits. Private great rooms, baths, kitchens, sitting rooms and trappings more common to the finest hotels created the special ambiance of the facility. In those days, an invitation to the apartments was a very exciting proposition.

Those influenced by Alan Dorhmann's work included Dr. Edward Deming, Walt Disney, Alexander Everett, Tom Wilhite, Warner Erhardt, John Hanley, Bill Dempsey, William Penn Patrick, Michael Murphy, Richard Nixon, John F. Kennedy, Clement Stone, Jane Wilhite, Leland Val Van De Wall, and many leaders in the field of human progress.

Alan Dohrmann presided with the authority of a Pope and the magic of a leprechaun over his family of nine children: Terry, Pam, Bernhard, Mark, Geof, Melissa, Carl, Susan and Sally. The lessons included in this book are only a sample of the many more that Alan Dohrmann imparted to his beloved family during their growing years.

The pioneering breakthroughs created by the Alan Dohrmann and those he chose to work beside, continue to reach millions of individuals even now. In 1983, he passed on, or "graduated," as he liked to call it.

. . . And to All a Good-Night

Once upon a time, a four-year old, blue-eyed, blonde-haired baby child woke up and walked out into a hallway that led to a family Christmas tree, dragging his favorite binki behind him. It was exactly midnight.

Squinting from the sudden burst of lights, he spied an elf man with a pipe —his father, coming into focus, balancing on a ladder. The elf man seemed to be trying to re-hang a Christmas ornament that Circe, one of the five Persian cats, had playfully adopted earlier as a toy. Such adoptions from the famous Dohrmann Christmas tree were not uncommon.

Dohrmann Christmas trees were a special tradition in the family, and the decorating party usually involved all the members of the Dohrmann clan that lived nearby. The tree was famous in the neighborhood because it was one of the largest. The 1952 Dohrmann Christmas tree was almost twenty-two feet high, with room for the large angel on the top near the ceiling cross beam.

Mr. Dohrmann was carefully repositioning the cat's chosen

ornament on one of the highest boughs. On the far side of the room, unseen by the little boy, was a Benedictine monk sipping hot cocoa.

As the small boy entered the room, wiping sleep from his half-opened eyes, I tingled with a *knowing* that this moment, this little drama about to unfold, was the reason I was here for the winter holidays. At times, God sends an angel to tap us on the shoulder, a sort of heavenly heads-up when something special is coming.

The little boy entered and glared at his father, a drowsy glare, but a glare nonetheless. Father was wasting precious time. Santa might come at any moment and find the room occupied. Who knew what catastrophe might ensue? He might not even come down the chimney. Look at that blazing hearth! Visions of a singed Santa danced in his sleepy head.

His father switched on his largest smile, as his head turned from the ornament he held in his hand, to face the boy. The boy shuffled his feet, occasionally jerking a foot across the path of the ill-fated comforter that trailed behind him. A bit tattered for indoor-outdoor wear, the binki literally went everywhere the boy went, which was now a place near the foot of the ladder to one side of the roaring fire.

A sleepy set of very blue eyes matched the fire with their heat, and a twin pair stared back down from a very high ladder. As if the two had already been engaged in an extended conversation, Mr. Dohrmann "continued" speaking from some point he just left a moment ago. The large frosted ornament that he still held in his hand reflected his image, multi-colored from the lights of the tree. From my hiding place in the shadows of the room I could see Mr. Dohrmann's expressions in the reflecting orb as he spoke.

"You know, Bee . . ." pipe clenched between his teeth, Mr. Dohrmann steadied himself on the ladder and twirled the sparkling bulb between his fingers, "some folks think all these bulbs are real and they hang on this tree to decorate the branches. Is that what YOU think, Bee?"

"Dunno, Dad." (Always a safe answer.) If I leaned over and around, I could see that Bee's answer was muted by the insertion of his thumb, for a bit of security sucking, much like a nervous student wondering if the test was coming. The sleepy four-year-old mind was not certain about the importance that any question could have at midnight, especially on the night that had only one purpose relating not to questions, but to SANTA CLAUS. Bee wanted his Dad to damp the fire and go

to sleep so that Santa would not be frightened off. He wished
his brothers and sisters were here to help.

But his father went on talking. "As I'm looking with my
magic eyes, what I see from up here, Bee, is not just ONE
ornament. Nope, what I can see, if I look really really hard
into this one ornament, the only one that Circe chose to play
with on the floor . . ." And now he put his face up close to the
ornament, staring into it . . . "I see the dark hallway reflected
in back of you, and the movement that took place when you
stepped into our Christmas room."

The boy looked back over his shoulder.

Mr. Dohrmann twisted the bulb as if this would give him
a better view. "Yep," he continued, "I see magic here, Bee.
Because I have always known something special about our
family Christmas tree. Do you know what that something
special is, Bee? What do you think is special about our family
Christmas tree?"

The giant elf leaned back on his ladder to look down upon
the boy, who replied in a sleepy sing-song voice, "The tree is
filled with our memories, Dad?"

"That's right, Bee. That's the answer. Only there's more
to it. This tree is filled with our memories, and because it was

filled past the *critical point* — the critical point, Bee . . . this Christmas tree IS ALIVE. I select each tree for our family, every Christmas, using all the power I have, Bee, so that I can seek and find the most ALIVE of all Christmas trees to place inside our home. Did you know this is how it is done?

Shaking his head. No, he did not know.

"And do you know why?" his father's gaze still fixed on the giant frosted magical orb.

The boy, sitting partly on his binki and partly on the hardwood floor amidst reflections that like tiny fireflies in summer skittered all around him, again sent his father the NO signal with his head. "Dunno Dad," a sleepy voice that sounded like all of this was a dream — a room with a blazing fire-place, a sparkling Christmas tree and a father who was only a dreamy illusion — coming from a pre-Santa reverie "almost" remembered.

"I'll tell you why," his father continued excitedly, commanding firm attention with another twist on the bulb, as if the rear side held an entirely new view. "Magic is waiting for ALL OF US, Bee, waiting for us all in lots of ways. You can only see my LIVING ornament ONE WAY from so far down where you sit. But from up here, Bee, it's not a big frosted crystal ornament at all. Why, it's actually a WINDOW . . . a magic WINDOW into a world that is more real than anything we think we know. It's more like the world I know you children live in, each and every day!

"In my CRYSTAL world," he held the ornament in both hands, his elbows on the top of the ladder, and stared as if in some trance induced by fairies, "Bee, I can see our fireplace and all the Christmas lights that are now spilling and twinkling all over our floor." Mr. Dohrmann spun the ornament, staring at first one quarter, then another.
"Why, I can see the aliveness of the tree in the back light of the fire. I can see the true TREE Bee, the Tree that is really ALIVE, from up here.

And the boy was standing now to get a better look, with his own hand on the ladder as he stretched his gaze.

"I can see, Bee, that every branch has a magic white light filled with all the memories of our family. Each and every branch, Bee." Mr. Dohrmann's voice caught in his throat, as if life were happening to him for the very first time this Christmas Eve. I noticed that Forest, by the side wall with a linen towel over his arm, was watching the drama in rapt attention.

Mr. Dohrmann continued with his Christmas story. "In fact, wait a minute. Yes . . . YES . . . every NEEDLE has the light of LIFE . . . and the needles are LAUGHING. Yes, they are LAUGHING . . . because they are so happy you and your brothers and sisters took the time to honor their life, and to decorate them so that GOD would see how happy they were when serving our family and adding their light to our Christmas.

"Their life light, Bee, is so bright . . . so very bright, and it jumps off every needle and kisses every other object in the room, Bee. I wish you could see. I wish you could see . . . how the needle light flows off every end point like tiny fingers to blend into all the light sources all over the room. For in the crystal ball, Bee, everything, everything I see at Christmas is just another light source. A source light for God, like some magic playground . . . all lit up."

More spinning of the ornament, and intense staring . . . "I can see reflections of Mom and all the kids still lingering here inside, as they giggle and make the popcorn strings, and place the tinsel up high and down low. I can even FEEL it, Bee. I can FEEL the spirit of CHRISTMAS here. It's leaping and spinning out of this magic place . . ."

He shook his head as if in wonder and disbelief, but we both could tell it WAS real, from the way he looked even harder. His whole being simply confirmed that what he was seeing and saying to us was REAL, and everything else was UNREAL.

"Bee . . . wait . . . I can see you coming out of the dark place in the hall. And yes, you are SHOWERED in Magical Red and Green and Blue and White and all the colored lights from the Christmas Tree. But you are so bright. You seem to have a light from the fire behind you that is flowing off you in all directions.

"Wait!" Mr. Dohrmann pressed his face to what seemed like the inside of the frosted ornament, as he held his gaze only an eyelash away from the glazed bulb, surrounded by fiery reflective light. "WAIT A MINUTE!!!!"

The boy was frozen in total attention now, his head arched back and his eyes wide as saucers, so involved had he become in his father's Christmas story. Mr. Dohrmann moved the ornament very low, because he knew the boy was not completely certain if his father was telling the truth. One step at a time, as if he were carrying the most precious treasure in the Universe, always staring mystified into the depth of the giant Frosted, Twirling Orb protected by a father's big, strong hands. One proud step at a time, down the ladder . . .

Step. Down. Step. Down.

Step carefully with one hand holding on . . . step finally off the ladder . . . one last foot (big as Santa and just as round) . . . *Bang!* It landed on the hardwood floor.

Slippers reaching to an inch of where the boy now stood staring up . . . squatting again, his binki circled around him . . . He pulled the binki closer for further protection as he gazed into the depths of the magic sphere his father was holding between them. Four eyes staring into a wonderland of magic.

Mr. Dohrmann squatted down even lower into lotus position, next to the four-year-old, as if he were another child and this was the most natural thing in the world to do with children at midnight on Christmas Eve. Then, stretching out his arm, Mr. Dohrmann held the orb in front of the boy's eyes, so the Christmas Tree was on one side and the fireplace was behind them.

"The Christmas Ornament distorts light and image and creates its own world, Bee. Do you see YOUR OWN LIGHT IN THE CHRISTMAS WORLD?" Again, he spun the globe.

"I see it, Dad." The sleepy voice was waking up now and the child's blue eyes held a fascination only the best teachers in the world will ever really experience.

"It's MAGIC, Bee, this light that God has put around you."

Forest and I both were transfixed, focused on father and son, who were seeing and feeling THE LIGHT together, at midnight.

The next day the boy would tell me that he saw inside this bright frosted ornament the most amazing sights. He told me, as naturally as if it were the story of putting on his shoes, that the fire had cast a light that ran off every part of his tiny young body. A light that flowed like foxfire in back-lit illumination, and spilled forward to mix with the twinkle and sparkle of the Christmas tree lights. He told me that he could see that everything in the room was really alive with light, and that everything in the Christmas room had its own color, its own light, that pulsed and glowed. The mantelpiece. Every table and chair. Every inch of carpet. But the most intense lights were flowing from the Christmas Tree and from his father and himself, he explained. These lights would reach out to touch one another.

He felt it was like hugging. He said there was no fear anywhere in the lights. He said he always would see these lights at Christmas time, he was sure of it. But this came later.

At the time there were four eyes, a little space, and a frosted ornament in an oversized protective palm.

". . . The real Magic, Bee, is YOU at Christmas time. Oh, I told you all about the Magic of Christmas many times, but down deep in your heart you don't have room to FEEL the REAL magic sometimes.

"I know. I KNOW this is true.

"So as your father, I want you to FEEL that the lessons your Dad has given to you, each time you hear one of your father's stories, are more important than all the Christmas presents under all the Christmas trees in all the world."

"Bee, many children don't have a father to tell them stories at Christmas time, or at any time. And for the millions of children who do have a father, somehow, somewhere, along the way of a father's life, their MAGIC burned itself out, Bee. For these children never receive a father's story. Not even once!"

At this point, Mr. Dohrmann, even more fixed on his Globe of Magic, without another word, gently, without the boy's knowing or thinking about it . . . the father lifted a tiny arm and stretched little fingers . . . and he placed the ornament into those two little hands for the very first time. As he did so,

he began to feel all around the boy, patting the air as if
something around the boy could be moved into proper position.

While Mr. Dohrmann's hands moved around the outline
of the boy, feeling all around him without touching him, he
continued to stare into the magic ornament. The father traced
his son's entire three-dimensional being in the firelight, the
reflected light in the WONDERLAND ORB that was flowing
from behind, like fingers of the aurora stream off the Northern
Lights, jagged and pulsing, rippling and surrounding the boy's
entire body with colors, mixed with the lights and colors of
Christmas . . . very much ALIVE!

The boy began to notice that when his father moved his
small hands for him, the light moved also. The light raced and
shot from each tiny finger, reached out and touched the tree
light and connected to the light of all the needles, each one on
fire . . .

And as I watched the two, I could also see for the first
time, that the tree did have Life Lights, as Mr. Dohrmann
would call them later. And the LIFE LIGHT was surrounding
every NEEDLE just like he had told us. You could see it so
clearly in the ornament's reflection.

Then the father's free hand grasped the tip of one of the

boughs that was closest, to move it up and down, whimsically. And the light from the needles shot forward and grabbed hold of the reflected light that was shooting off the boy's fingers. For a moment, the communication in the room HELD and became an actual FEELING . . . a tingling.

A feeling of ONENESS with all creation. A feeling of all things being connected. And we watched the boy turn his hands in amazement as he saw the light shimmering over his arms and out from his fingers to touch and become ONE with the light from the LIVING Christmas Tree. Yes, it was magic . . .

At this point, I held out my own hands and started looking at them as they caught the essence of this light source that was zooming around the room and connecting every object with a single magic orb, the Christmas ornament held in the hands of a tiny boy at midnight.

"This is the LIGHT of CHRISTMAS, my son." He smiled down at him, " . . . and it is always the LIGHT OF GOD. For all living things to be SEEN, they also must REFLECT the LIGHT of the LORD. However, only a special FEW in life can ever see the true wonderful light of Christmas. So few have the sight. So few. Most will never find the truth we feel and see this Christmas, Bee. These will never see, never know.

"But the Christmas Light is always here, all the same, always touching them, for it matters not whether they see the LIGHT of CHRISTMAS. The needles of life are always ALIVE as are all sights in our Christmas world. And each will always be laughing in their own true service to God, and to each other.

"One of the Ornaments each year, usually only ONE, Bee, will become your magic window to the true inner light of Christmas. But the real MAGIC, my son, is YOU. For what you can't know is a father's feeling on this night. And for your father, the only gift that you could possibly bring to me that would fill my heart so completely full, is the vision of MY SON and HIS LIFE FORCE touching the MAGIC LIGHT of CHRISTMAS as together we are sitting here on the floor, a son and his Dad at midnight, and KNOWING that MY son can SEE the one true LIGHT of Christmas with me . . .

"You, my son, represent a great LIGHT in my life, and the light you see this Christmas Eve, is only ONE of the many lights of Christmas.

"There are eight more lights in your brothers and sisters, and your mother is a huge light that fills the room like the sun. As all these lights come into our Christmas room, whether they know it or not . . . the Light of Christmas, this Christmas, our Christmas, flows off their hands and fingers and faces and feet as it spreads around the room to touch and mingle and become ONE LIGHT. And in this Christmas time when all our lights become only ONE.

"We are so lucky, Bee, because we have a real magic here that we call our Family . . .the lesson being that FAMILY is a blending of our lights, yours and mine . . . your mom's and your brothers' and your sisters' . . . Forest's and Brother Al's and all our Family Lights . . . just as you discovered this Christmas in a magic orb that hangs high on a special family Christmas tree.

"This is the one present you can unwrap all your life, Bee. The gift of your family and the light that is contained inside. A light to shelter, protect, guide and nurture in all the Christmases to come . . . enriched by your family MEMORIES."

Then Mr. Dohrmann wiggled back on the floor, behind the boy. "Don't turn!" he instructed, as little Bee started to twist around. His father lifted both of his great hands over the boy's head and held out the MAGIC ORB in front of the four-year-old's eyes. Once again, he began to turn it.

As Bee told it later, he remembered the image exploded into two silvery silhouettes, two auras, two blended beings of light and color moving and expanding, shimmering together and becoming one light.

"The real Magic is that YOU, my SON, are the LIGHT within ME for all my Christmases . . . all the Christmases I have known or ever will know. For all our light together is the LIGHT OF THE LORD, and it is this truth that is the Spirit of my Christmas." He twirled the orb in front of his son, and for moments that seemed like an eternity, the two sat, holding their arms and fingers entwined, in silence. Bee remembers he touched the ball once or twice. He remembered that as he turned to look up, his teacher was crying.

I recall how Bee reached up to hug his father . . . and I recall how he looked in those great arms, as the Master tightly held his oldest boy. Was it the boy or the monk that was now four years old? The sight of them was nearly blinding. I had to look away; the tenderness of the moment was so intense, so private.

At last I turned to see the boy moving back down the hall with its dark forbidding fringes. I could see Mr. Dohrmann once again on the ladder as if the entire evening had never taken place. He took one last look at his first-born son before putting the frosty Christmas ball carefully back upon the tree.

Then he said, to no one in particular, "KNOW how Christmas FEELS, my son. Go to sleep now and dream about the living lights of memory. But, Bee, NEVER forget our Christmas story . . .

"For what is important is not how Christmas looks to others. The lesson is how you and you alone will KEEP the FEELING of Christmas. Tonight is only one memory, wrapped as a gift from a tired old father for his eldest son. A gift that you may one day, many years later, open each and every Christmas, to knowingly look inside, and to SEE, once again, the true LIGHTS OF CHRISTMAS.

"Now, everyone . . . take the FEELING of CHRISTMAS...and go to sleep. Santa Claus is coming . . ."

Circe, the cat, curled into a corner of the large overstuffed sofa, yawned and stretched, and immediately went back to sleep.

Of Miracles and Magnets

It was a summer evening in 1959 and we had just finished dinner. I loved these evenings especially for their perfect temperature as the earth released the fragrances the sun had warmed, and the cooler breezes from the Bay gave just the right hint of tangy sea-scent. Now it was lesson time. Tiny feet trotted into the family room and the children settled in, forming their half-moon circle around their father.

Suddenly, Mr. Dohrmann let out a loud groan and with overly-exaggerated gestures, slowly he lifted his tired frame out of the chair. Then he walked behind his chair to the large sack that held the "story props" for the evening.

With great effort, Mr. Dohrmann half-dragged and half-slid the bag forward and around my feet, past Mrs. Dohrmann's chair and feet and positioned it in front of his own chair. The storyteller had achieved exactly what he had intended. All nine children were now eyeing the bag with great curiosity. What could be inside, that was so heavy?

"Ahhhhh!" With a long, loud sigh of relief, Mr. Dohrmann settled into his soft chair once again. Then, pretending not to pay attention to anyone else in the room, he lowered his hands deep into the large "story sack." The bag bulged this way and that as he moved his hands inside the sack. Finally, he looked up, smiled at the family, and withdrew his hands from the sack.

We saw that he had tied a cord to each of his index fingers. At the end of each cord, dangling and swinging freely, were two large silver spheres. Each sphere was just slightly smaller than the size of a grapefruit, and they were highly polished. The reflection of the entire family danced on their surfaces. The two spheres dangled like mirrors showing off the cloudy sky and mountain backdrop through the open, ceiling-high windows that lined the far wall of the lesson room.

"Children, do you know what I am holding in my hands?" After much whispering and giggling, Terry said, "Two silver balls on two cords, Dad?"

Mr. Dohrmann frowned, and we knew the answer was wholly inadequate.

"But what about the silver balls, Terry? What makes them unique?"

Again, some further whispering and coaching. Pam, the next oldest, raised her hand. "Father, the two balls are identical?"

A beaming smile from Mr. Dohrmann. "Yes, children, each of my silver spheres IS precisely identical Even more than you may ever suspect.

"But that is not the lesson."

He jerked first one ball and then the other so that it would swing like a pendulum back and forth and connect to the other with a WHACK.

WHACK.

WHACK.

"You see, children, while teaching over at the University, I had the Bureau of Standards and Measures work on each of these two spheres. In fact, I chose them especially for our lesson tonight. Do you know why?"

WHACK!

Tiny heads shaking no.

"Because Children, each sphere, the one on my left and the one on my right, is the same. Exactly the same!"

WHACK!

"In every way, the same!"

WHACK!

"The weight of both spheres is the same."

WHACK.

"The circumference of both spheres is the same."

WHACK.

"The number of molecules in each sphere is the same."

WHACK.

"The number of atoms in each sphere is the same."

WHACK!!!!

"So children . . . what is DIFFERENT about ONE of my special spheres?"

I stared at each of the Silver Spheres. Like the children, I had no idea in the world what could be unique about one or the other.

After much nodding, Susan spoke. *"We don't know, Dad."* Of course, that was Mr. Dohrmann's favorite answer.

"Are you sure?" he asked each of them. He still held the spheres directly out in front of him, WHACKING them together every few seconds.

"We're sure, Dad."

Slowly, Mr. Dohrmann looked from one to the other and then moved his right hand higher, making the sphere on the right rise higher than the other one in his left hand. "Children...the sphere in my right hand is MAGNETIZED!"

As Mr. Dohrmann held the spheres closer without the energy to create a WHACK of separation, the spheres came together on their own accord.

Mr. Dohrmann pulled on his right hand until they came apart, and then placed the sphere suspended from his left hand back into the sack, untying the string from his finger. Then he extended his right hand once again, from which the magnetic sphere still dangled. "So children . . . what is different about the sphere on the right?"

Silence. Heads shaking.

"Children, would you like for me to tell you the answer?"
All heads nodding.

"Children, the magnet in my right hand contains properties that physicists describe with great care. These scientists choose their words carefully. They use just the right words when they describe universal principles. The magnet is a universal principle, children. Although the sphere you are seeing now is exactly the same as the other sphere which is in the sack, it is also unique. Why?

"Remember: Physicists choose their words VERY precisely, children, and physicists say that the magnetized sphere — and they don't say in their words that the sphere CREATES or that the sphere GENERATES — rather they say that the sphere on the right DISPLAYS a *Power*. And the power being displayed is the POWER of ATTRACTION. This power RADIATES in all directions, always with the same force. It attracts all objects, in equal manner, that fall into its POWER.

". . .But that IS NOT the lesson . . .

"So tell me, children, why are YOU like the sphere on my right?"

Susan again, with, "We don't know, Dad."

"You're sure?"

Little heads nodded in unison.

"Let us look into WHY the sphere in my right hand DISPLAYS a *POWER*. Even though the sphere in my right hand is exactly the same as the sphere my left hand held, the only difference is the fact that the sphere in my right hand was MAGNETIZED.

"But what does this mean? The answer IS that the sphere in my right hand has all its MOLECULES in alignment." Mr. Dohrmann nodded to Mrs. Dohrmann, and she held up a large photo book with an illustration of the molecules in perfect alignment, as opposed to randomly displayed molecules.

Mr. Dohrmann continued.

"And I believe my children are like MAGNETS of GOD using universal principles. I believe that my children, each one of you . . ." He walked around the half moon, holding the sphere in front of each child's face, while he stood behind them, so each could see themselves in the perfect reflection of the magnetized sphere, " . . . are individual little MAGNETS for GOD.

"You, my children, are magnets. And I believe . . ." Mr. Dohrmann settled back in his chair, holding the sphere in front of him, " . . . that YOU display a *POWER*. When you become adults, things may not always go just the way you want them to, inside your life." Mr. Dohrmann swung a circle in the air with his sphere, as a symbol of the circle of the life each child would pass through. I noticed that the lights from the candles were becoming brighter as the room darkened. They began to add their own dance to the reflection on the surface of the silver sphere.

"You may have all sorts of unforeseen challenges along the adult journey of your lives. Challenges your mother and I could never imagine, as we look upon you this night. And through these times, your mother and I, although you can't imagine it today, may no longer be here to make it safe for you, or to make the bad things go away. You will have to deal with challenges in your life, one-by-one, all by yourself. Even your brothers and sisters may not be around to help you on the day that you need help the most." Heads turned back and forth as they looked at each other.

"For you see, children, when things are not going just the way you desire, I ask that you remember the lesson, on this evening, with your father and mother and Brother Al and our family intact together. Remember the lesson of the spheres. And when you have challenges, I want you to look INSIDE rather than OUTSIDE, as to what might be the cause of each challenge.

"I want you to look INSIDE to see if the molecules inside YOU are in ALIGNMENT with the will of GOD. I want you to test the power of your own surrender to God. I want my children to hear the WHACK that flows from having all their molecules in perfect alignment with the will of God.

"Are your molecules in ALIGNMENT with the values we have shared here, inside this family? Are your molecules in ALIGNMENT with GOD and the values you have been taught? Are your FEELING molecules in ALIGNMENT right now? Are your WORD molecules in ALIGNMENT? Are your

ACTION molecules in ALIGNMENT?

"For I believe, children, you will always find that if you fail to receive what you most desire in life, you will also discover somewhere on the inside, your molecules are OUT OF ALIGNMENT. And if you will put your molecules back into alignment, I also believe you WILL display a POWER. And the power will be the power of divine attraction.

"As you manifest all that is good and wholesome and perfect about your lives and your future, as you share your problems in life as brothers and sisters all growing up together, I want each of you to always, always look first to the INSIDE and ask one another — Are your molecules in DIVINE ALIGNMENT?

"For if they are, if YOU ARE . . .

YOU *WILL* DISPLAY A *POWER!*

"Now run off to bed . . . like powerful little magnets!"

The Concept of Oneness

That last Thanksgiving was like a summons. Mrs. Dohrmann had alerted my Abbot that most certainly, because of the nature of Mr. Dohrmann's illness, this was likely to be the last Thanksgiving for him. I had been cordially invited to join the entire family for the Thanksgiving feast. It was 1982. The Dohrmanns had moved from the Fairfax estate and were now living in a two-story, wonderful place of light in Greenbrae. Wide vistas of San Francisco Bay with sweeping views of Mount Tamalpais made each window a master's landscape.

The family arrived from the many states in which they lived. The nine had their own children, "ankle-biters," Mr. Dohrmann called them. Always, he had tireless energy for them.

Throughout the dinner, we avoided mention of how he looked. The chemotherapy had taken a huge toll and four surgeries had not stopped the ravages of cancer. Still, he was beaming. "No pain, no gain," he joked lightly. He wore a

Parisian artist's beret on top of his injured, hairless head and faked the energy for every grandchild. The elders knew it was sorely taxing for him.

After the feast, everyone retired into the large living room where the Master played a thrilling performance on his grand piano. When he was finished, with the help of his cane, he hobbled over to the same giant chair that the Fairfax home had made so memorable to all of us. Sitting alone and facing us, with his back to the fireplace . . . ignoring the advice of legions of doctors one more time, he tamped down and lit his inseparable companion, a favorite meershaum pipe, and smiled.

"Are you children all ready for a lesson?" he beamed, looking down at the ankle-biters in the half-moon circle before him and ignoring his own nine, sitting in sofas and chairs behind them.

Tiny heads nodded. "Yes, Grandpa."

"Good. That's good . . . because the lesson is ready for YOU!"

He rose and brought several large brown "story bags" from behind his chair, much to the delight of the little ones on the floor.

I noticed a circle of candles had been lit around the

circumference of the room, and the light was now playing on the white furniture and walls. Reaching into the large brown "story bags," he began to take out . . . shoes.

Shoes of all different colors, sizes and shapes, which he proceeded to arrange on the carpet in front of us.

"Can any of you tell me what is the SAME about all these shoes?" Holding his cagey smile in check as once again he seemed absorbed solely in the tamping of his pipe.

A good deal of discussion ensued, including substantial study of the shoes.

"We don't know what's the same about the shoes," said more than one grandchild. "They all look different to us, Grandfather."

"Yes, well, that is not the lesson is it? Let me tell you what makes these shoes the same . . . which is the featured content of tonight's lessons.

"I am sure you all know, simply to make the doctors right, as they so hate to be wrong, this is probably my last Thanksgiving. I want to thank you all for making it also, MY BEST.

"I love you all so. And knowing the end is coming, I thought I'd better tidy up some things . . . important things. Things I don't want forgotten when I am gone. Things like my prayer center for ONENESS that we started a few years ago. Remember when our family and a few friends were the only members?" He looked at his children, receiving confirming nods from them.

"Well the prayer centers for ONENESS now operate in thirty-two countries, children. Did you KNOW that?"

Little heads shook, "No, Granddad."

"Well, they DO. And it all started right here in San Francisco. For our guests, let me explain. The Prayer Centers for ONENESS meet in a chosen house of worship for a different religion once a month, every month. Leaders from every congregation and denomination are invited to attend. The meetings take two hours. Meetings include a group prayer at the beginning and end. Everyone sits in circles, and in larger meetings there are many circles. One person starts and everyone shares around the circle. But what do they share?"

"They share one idea that is THE SAME about the faiths of the world, Grandpa?"

"That's right, perfect! The Prayer centers on ONENESS – It focuses on what is the SAME about each faith. And no one thinks about anything that is different, for at least two short hours.

"As it is likely to be my very last Thanksgiving, it is also likely to be my very last PRAYER meeting on Oneness. So I asked my twin brother Jerry to take me to the San Francisco Center last Sunday for ONENESS.

"Which brings me to the story of these shoes in front of you tonight."

The candlelight highlighted the many colors and varieties of the vast array of shoes.

"Your Uncle Jerry fussed over me like some damaged bird-ling! Finally, we arrived at the Muslim mosque, the site of this Sunday's ONENESS service. As your Uncle Jerry and I were preparing to enter, I noticed an elderly woman, who was grumbling and obviously changing her mind about attending this month's Oneness Service.

"I went over and introduced myself, to inquire if I might help." Mr. Dohrmann was drawing mightily on his pipe, which had come alive like a dragon with his tale.

"I came to find the woman was a delightful Jewish mother who was attending her first Oneness Session at the insistence of her son. She complained that all this ONENESS mumbo-jumbo was lost on her. She was eighty-two, 'for crying out loud,' as she phrased it! She had a religion that for five thousand years already had it right, starting virtually every prayer with PRAISED BE THE LORD, GOD IS ONE. Why did she need THIS to tell her about Oneness? Why did her SON think she needed this?

"Then she had to come halfway 'cross town, to this Holy MUSK — I corrected her, telling her it was MOSK(QUE) — and she didn't see anything really all that much Holy about it, either.

"And now her son, already inside, was waiting to meet her. When she arrived, she gathered from all the shoes on the mats by the door, that she was supposed to enter with her shoes off. So she had decided, 'Not today, buddy boy!' — and proceeded to enter the MOSK with her shoes on.

"However, the sharp clicking noises of her heels brought on criticisms from the security persons inside the MOSK, who forced her back outside, until she took her shoes off. Oh, she had taken her shoes off. But she was now putting them back on.

"This was ridiculous.

"This was not for her.

"I had sat down beside her, listening intently. And as she

was putting her shoes on, I was taking mine shoes off."

"'So are you going to this ONENESS THING?' she asked him curiously.

"I looked at her and said, 'I thought I'd give it a try, Mrs. Silverstein. You may have noticed I'm not doing too well in the health department these days. That's my twin brother, Jerry Dohrmann, over there; now, he is the healthy one. I want you to meet him!'

"Mrs. Silverstein shook hands with Jerry, who already had his shoes off, and was on his way into the mosque.

"'Mrs. Silverstein,'" I continued, "' there is a lesson here somewhere. See all these shoes. They are all different. Different sizes. Different colors. Different ways of putting on and taking off. When a man is dying, Mrs. Silverstein, he begins to feel the whole world is a Holy place. This mosque, the street over there, a park . . . taking off my shoes is the easy part. FINDING OUT why so many different pairs of shoes might be alike in some way is God's mystery. Perhaps you came here today to TEACH rather than to learn. Did you ever think of that?'"

"Mrs. Silverstein looked at me, sitting on the mat for a few moments, and then she sat down herself and took off her shoes. Together, arm in arm, we walked into the mosque.

"Looking back on it, children, it must have been very new for Mrs. Silverstein. She was bent over, in her black mourning dress, hardly looking at the huge columns rising to the sky. It was so quiet. The rumblings of small discussions roared like distant thunder from somewhere in the belly of the vast interior of the ageless mosque. It was a long walk for Mrs. Silverstein. As she took her place in the great circle of ONENESS service that day, she looked up, lifted the veil from her hat, and said with penetrating eyes, 'Thank you, Mr. Dohrmann.' Then she faced the group and her son with resolve.

"Staring back at her, she would find a Catholic priest, a friendly rabbi, a Baptist minister, various Protestant ministers, Evangelical preachers, deacons, Buddhist monks, a Hindu Brahmin priest, Muslim mullahs, and Native American shamans. One Hawaiian kahuna sat next to Mrs. Silverstein.

"And it began. Everyone sharing a ritual of ONENESS from their faith, that united us all. Talk and prayer about what was the same in our humanness, our beliefs.

"A young woman who had passed us to sit on my right, rose to share. She had tears in her eyes, obviously moved by the prayer work of the others, and she explained that in her liturgy, the chant was the message. She felt compelled to share her gift of CHANTING with our Oneness family. After this short explanation, she broke into rocking back and forth, and chanting in the most magical musical manner. Her song filled the mosque for almost ten minutes.

"There was no applause when she was finished.

"There were no words for her song.

"Many in the circles had been moved to tears, so powerful and uplifting was the voice with which she had blessed us all.

"Then it was time to complete the circle, and it was Mrs. Silverstein's turn to share. Someone helped her to her feet, and she turned and faced the group.

"There was a power in the way she slowly undid her veil and removed her small black hat. Placing the little hat in my lap, she undid a hairpin that let bands of long, gray hair fall to her shoulders, transforming her appearance. One could envision how lovely and special the younger Mrs. Silverstein had been, to even now command such fineness in her sharp features.

"Gazing directly at her son, halfway across the circle, she lifted her bony hand and pointed at him like some witch from

Oz.

"'HIM . . .

"'If not for HIM ... I would not have attended your service for ONENESS.

"'After all, I am eighty-two.

"'You are just children.

"'I feel like the only adult in the room.'

"Then moving her withered arthritic hand in my direction, she pointed down to me.

"'AND HIM. If he had not been kind enough to share a few corrective words with an old woman at the door, my shoes would still be on my feet, and I would be walking far away from here.

"'However, as it is, I arrived, no accidents, and I'm here, because of HIM and HIM.' And she pointed again.

"'Then as you all shared, I thought how irrelevant all the information is.

"'That the information you share here won't change anything. Not even one point of view. A human condition forged through generations of focusing attention, RELIGIOUS attention, only on WHAT IS DIFFERENT about each of us.

"'Like some Lilliputian story, where one society slaughters

another because their headgear is different. One wears pots and pans. One wears vegetables on their heads. Or where one society performs the racial cleansing because one society opens its eggs from the small end at the top rather than then large end at the bottom. Or a society where six million Jews are slaughtered because they read a book from back to front and wear a little hat when they pray.

"'I thought as you all went around the circle with your words, "Look for what is the essence here. After all, they have been meeting for years. They know some things. Find their essence and see if you can understand the truth within it."

"'I had about given up searching for such truth from all the various words and sincere sharings. I could only see you all picking up, going back, each into your different worlds, having very little new to take with you that was truly the SAME.

"'In fact, when this young lady here began to chant, I thought, "Here it comes. The reason to rise up and leave altogether" because all the feeling of what was different came crashing over me.

"'And I was not alone in my feelings, you see.

"'Oh, I saw it on your face, Rabbi, and you too, Mr. Baptist

Minister.

"'The patience of the monks was also tried, as you blocked out your feelings to retain a focus for what was real and true about our circle.

"'But then, during her long chant, something quite profound came over me.

"'While you were watching her, I looked up. And as I did, I noticed the most pure white dove was hovering, without its wings flapping at all, just there.' And she pointed to the great dome of the mosque, open to a morsel of sky.

"'I watched the Dove as if the bird were suspended by the psalm notes of the young lady's chant . . . floating for an eternity above our heads.

"'It created a profound feeling for me.

"'When I looked down again, I almost gasped. For somehow my eyes had in their new focus of light, failed to reel you all back in. For when I looked back down all I could see were feet.

"'I thought, "Well, it's dark here, and there is a dust stirring in the shallow sunlight." I looked around the circle and the focus of my attention was on your feet.

"'Of course, you must remember how tiny this old Jewish widow woman is. My eyes were almost at the level of your feet already.

"'However, I came to understand, as the chant was rushing over me, that my soul was doing the looking for me.

"'For the question that was being asked of me was profound. I was being asked, as if from the DOVE, as if a voice commanded me to reply — "Where is the Jewish foot? Where are the Baptist feet in this circle? Where is a Buddhist foot? Where is a Protestant foot? Where is a Catholic foot? Where is Muslim foot?"

"'I looked around the feet that seemed to be staring me straight in the face.

"'As I looked, I went around the circle more than once . . . looking only at the feet.

"'A circle of feet ... all pointing towards me.

"'I heard the voice again, "Where is the foot you seek?"

"'As the chant continued, I began to notice tears had come into my eyes.

"'For I found that in this room, it was impossible to find the difference that was before me.

"'What I found was — what was THE SAME about the circle.

"'It may have been my imagination, but when I chose to

next look up, the white Dove was still hovering. My eyes found the bird hovering directly in the sun spot above us. I had to squint and shade my eyes to see. Still the chant rose.

"'The instant my eyes fixed on the bird, its wings began to move and it lifted over the mosque . . . hovered only a second more, and was gone. However, as it drifted over the lip of the mosque, a huge voice seemed to call within me; it said:

"'THE LORD GOD SEES ONLY FEET.'"

"'Again I looked at the feet in the room, as our young lady completed her chant. And as I looked, I kept chanting, "The Lord God sees Feet, the Lord God sees only feet."

"'I next considered how we in our human view put so much more into our vision. We begin as we place our shoes upon our feet, to make each FOOT that God is seeing in his ONENESS as different as we can make it.

"'Then we place our different clothings and trappings upon ourselves, so that even our appearance is as different as we can make it.

"'We invest so little of life THINKING of what is the magnificent SAME about each and every one of us. That which binds us.

"'Yet wherever we go, wherever we journey in life, we move

toward our destinations as ONE, using our FEET to transport us to the place we seek. If our feet are damaged, we use our hands. Then the Lord God sees only HANDS.

"So I suppose if a newcomer has anything to share with you, a non-believer — it is this:

"'As you leave this mosque, and place your shoes upon your feet . . .

"'Whenever you are in your churches, your offices, your cars . . .

"'Your streets, your stadiums, your shopping malls . . .

"'Whenever you are alone or in groups, and your spirit tells you to be calm, to visit with your God, perhaps you might begin your prayer, your thoughts that the LORD GOD IS ONE.

"'With the memory of our circle on this Sunday, beside some very magic men and women, and an old, broken 82-year-old lady who has, with hardly any eyesight at all, imagined she heard some angels call her, and created the illusion of a very particular white dove that delivered an intuition, an inspiration, an inner truth for knowing, that indeed . . .

"'THE LORD GOD SEES ONLY FEET.

"'And if we all can hold our vision on our FEET perhaps, yes, perhaps . . . we will come to worship together as we learn to know . . .

"'THE LORD GOD *IS* ONE!

"'And the circle is complete.'"

 After pausing . . . smoking . . . staring . . . Mr. Dohrmann kneeled down and began to take each of the pairs of shoes and return them to the brown paper bag. Then a special thing happened. One of Mr. Dohrmann's youngest grandchildren, three years old, began to take off her shoes. She didn't say anything. She just took them off, walked over, put them into the bag and walked back to her place on the carpet.

Then another.

And another . . . until the nine and their children had all taken their shoes off . . . and the bag was so full, another was brought . . . and it was filled and removed. And the children and grandchildren sat with their feet toward their father and grandfather. Silently, he looked at them all.

And as he was looking, a very old lady dressed in black came out of Mr. Dohrmann's study. Very slowly, with hands gnarled and stiff with age, she unstrapped her shoes and took them off. Then, she sat down beside Mr. Dohrmann's easy chair. Slowly she stretched out her feet. And then, she reached over to take off Mr. Dohrmann's slippers, which she placed beside her shoes.

Then Mrs. Silverstein looked up and said to the children and grandchildren, "Happy Thanksgiving, Children.

" . . .and THAT is The Lesson . . ."

And as she held Mr. Dohrmann's hand, they brought out the pumpkin pie . . . to a perfect circle of FEET!

Thirty-One Flavors for the Soul

▅▅▅ In 1983, on a wonderfully fresh, warm winter afternoon in February, Mr. Dohrmann was dying. It had been an amazing time. The children were all present, and we had been retelling the "stories." Over a period of weeks, the old sage had fooled us and on many occasions, he had almost passed on.

The last time, he had been in a coma for six weeks. Father Frank Lacy, the family's favorite priest, had administered the last rites, and Frank was crying when he came out of the room.

However, Mr. Dohrmann didn't die. In fact, although we had to use a small crane to move him from his hospital bed in the large bedroom sitting area, he rested comfortably in his wheel chair. His eyes were sparkling as he emerged from the coma.

He could see his beloved Mount Tamalpais through his bedroom window, this mountain where he had loved to hike. He could see his Marin County and his San Francisco Bay where he had loved to sail. And he could survey all nine children and his many grandchildren, all sitting in front of him, as if a lesson were about to begin.

As Sally, the live-in nurse, finished feeding him a large bowl of ice cream, his favorite dessert, his face broke out in a large smile.

"Children," his very first word in six weeks, an elfin twinkle in his eyes, "you probably know that I have been ready to leave for a long, long time." He leaned forward in the wheel chair.

"If it were up to me, I would be serving on the other side this day.

"I have said good-bye, in my private way, to each and every one of you. And there really is nothing more I need to tell you. Some of you, I know, realize I have been gone far, far away these past many weeks, leaving you only with the idea you must get used to, that soon even this physical form will fade away, as the work continues on a higher plane.

"In fact, I want you all to embrace this idea with joy. After all I have taught you for long enough, it is now your time to teach, rather than study, the lessons."

He beamed at each of his precious children. They had come

from different parts of the country where they had made their homes, to be together with their father. And even as the time dragged on, they stayed for a period of weeks, waiting.

"Children," he chuckled, "you probably wonder why it is that I have come back at all?"

All heads nodding.

"There is a simple lesson in this 'coming back' that I wish for you to learn for everyday living.

"While I was offering my service on the other side, a thought came upon me that was so powerful, it restrained my ability to let go and pass forward into my next work. And the thought was this:

"Children . . . they simply do NOT have ICE CREAM over there. I have come back to have one MORE bowl of ICE CREAM!

"Today I have ordered that the doctors take off the life support, and as I place myself upon this swishing air bed you have created for me, I will sleep and remain this time in higher service. I only ask that you remain complete in all your dreams and memories for your father, knowing that in his life, the magic is, that when it came to ice cream, he, at the very end, had finally had just the right amount. It was enough. And like each flavor and every single scoop, you children with your gazes upon me now, are just like flavors of ice cream to my soul. For in my soul, so close now to the other side, I hold the taste of you, the color of your aura, the full measure of you all. And it is this, this INSIDE ICE CREAM that I will take with me when I do my higher work in just a little while from now.

"Now run off to be with your mother while they put me back to rest. And leave Bernhard with me, as I have one final lesson I wish for him to receive before I sleep; and Brother Al, you remain beside me too, as there are some words I wish to give to you as the family begins its new journey, in new ways, with my guidance expressed in new forms."

✍ Sally had helped him turn onto his side. His face was crushed into the down-soft pillows and his hands were spread through the rails of the hospital bed, as if pleading for human contact.

His son Bernhard, now thirty-five, came and sat beside his father, clasping his hands in his own. The two with identical blue eyes made from the same divine material, shared their moment of power as they gazed at each other. Then, Mr. Dohrmann began the last lesson:

Perfection
"CAN" Be Had!

"THESE ARE THE TEACHERS." His breathing was labored as he continued, FOR THESE

ARE THE TEACHERS.....staring directly into the eyes of his first-born son. "You know we have already said everything that needs to be said, Bee, don't you?"

"Yes, Dad," the young man responded.

"And you know that I have never shared my love with my children, one to the other, differently in any way."

"I know, Dad."

"And you know that I have always and forever loved my children equally and the same in every way?"

"Yes, Dad."

"And you know that your mother and I had yearned for many years to have a son, as the first four girls were born, isn't that correct?"

"Yes, Dad. I know."

"So I wanted to tell you in only this one small thing, it might be important for you to know later in your life . . . a little secret I felt you should share with Dad."

"What, Dad?"

"In this one small thing, Bee, and I know your mom joins me in this, which takes nothing from the other children . . .

We have always loved you FIRST. For you were our first son."

Tears splashed out of the young man's blue eyes, eyes so like his father's. No words, just tears. For the first time, the warrior Bee, who had led this family through the entire illness, was letting up and allowing himself to cry. As the tears dropped onto the bed sheet, Mr. Dohrmann looked at them, smiling. Then he took his index finger and softly traced the path of the tears on the young man's cheek. "But, Bee," he said, ". . .this is not the lesson . . ."

With great difficulty, Mr. Dohrmann continued, as if the story had no start or end. "I have made a magic life for us all, with all the children, but do you know why the magic is what it is, Bee?"

It was as if each breath were a victory, each word a conquest.

Bernhard shook his head.

"The magic has been the impossible circle of beings that have entwined our family AS the magic. Beings like Brother Al here," and he raised a weakened hand, attempting to point in my direction. But even this slight gesture was now too much for him. The hand fell back on his son's younger, stronger one. This was a sign to himself, to the three of us, that his strength was rapidly ebbing. My own eyes now smarting with tears, and I, too, let them flow freely.

"For you see, my *precious baby . . .*" From time to time, this name was used endearingly by Mr. Dohrmann for his son, a subject of great teasing from the others, " . . . .the greatest of THESE, that have lived among us, have been my many magic friends. My closest and bonded friendships.

"And of these, you have been surrounded all your life with their words, their presence, the power of their being. And without knowing it, you have been made more for it.

"For these of my friends that you have always known . . . have been the TEACHERS, Bee . . .

"And the teachers have come to us to SPREAD the TRUTH. To seize upon the truth as they know it to be, and to SPREAD the TRUTH to the students of the world, who need the truth like air. The students themselves will always appoint their own teachers, for the teachers rise from among the students in a timeless pageant for God's glory. Once so called, the teacher being true to his or her nature, moves within and creates their own destiny of service to the students of the world.

"And we, this family, have lived our lives within the presence of the greatest of these beings on the planet at this time, and we have known them as our Friends and Companions.

" . . . But . . . that is not the lesson . . .

"FOR THESE ARE THE MASTERS . . . FOR THESE ARE THE MASTERS.....

At this point, Bernhard brought his father's sipping cup to his lips. Without turning, Mr. Dohrmann took the straw in a mouth painted with white paste from medication and drawn with dying. I could see the oxygen was parching his mouth, leaving flakes around the corners. He sipped a moment and shook his head, indicating "enough," and they resumed their odd dance of eyes, this father and son.

Like chains dragging up anchors from a seabed, his words continued. "And of these Friends of our Family, my baby, there has been magic within magic. For from among these great beings, I have been blessed with my closest of all friends, those with whom I shared my confidences in this life.

"You have known them, one and all, but of these nearest to me, there were fewer. You have lived your life in privilege for the knowing of them. However, I realized in leaving you, that you did not have the words to speak of what it is you knew and felt. My returning here is about leaving you, at this time, the words for what it is you already know within yourself as a feeling, one for which you have no words.

"For the magic continues to be the honor the Lord God has bestowed upon us, to create our closest friendships among those with whom I have spent most of my time in this, my life's journey.

"Our closest friends.

"For my son . . . it is these friends that are known in this LIFE as the MASTERS!

"Masters who are chosen by their own students, the greatest of all the teachers. For in their graduation they, and only they, have come to this time to PROTECT the TRUTH from Error. Their students, the greatest of living teachers, will always recognize within their ranks, when the chosen are ready, the qualities of MASTERHOOD that shine in their midst. The teachers proclaim their MASTERS and the MASTERS recognize their own true nature from such a place of rejoicing, that they themselves are readied in the awakening.

"Masters are the rare ones. Masters are they who on this planet serve to ever vigilantly protect the TRUTH from Error. The Teachers rely upon their Masters to receive the truth in the form of eternity, and so recognizing the *error-free truth,* they rush to teach and instruct the perfect truth to their universe of students.

"Such is the Way of the pathway to the divine.

"And you, my son, have lived your life among the MASTERS." This was spoken with as much power as he could muster. Then, a pause.

The young man, still crying, gently squeezed his father's hand and nodded "yes" more than once.

"But that is not the lesson . . . THIS IS THE LESSON . . ."

"THE TEACHER OF MASTERS THE TEACHER OF MASTERS . . . A pause to regain breath, and then, like air rushing from a balloon, his voice a whisper, "For there are among these beings, the most rare of the rare . . . the highest of the high. And by these you have been transformed, merely by being in their presence.

"For these my son, have been during my life, my special reward for the walk I have chosen. These alone have been my ETERNAL FRIENDSHIPS, my FOREVER FRIENDS . . . my colleagues.

"So few, however . . . so FEW!

"So precious FEW!

"And none of these in the last have been my students, for

I have been a student OF THEM ALL . . ."

"You have lived your life among these as well. These beings of the Light . . .and you have not known who it was that mentored, tutored and loved you so.

"Oh, you have known the names. A Tom Wilhite or Warner, a John Hanley or Alexander Everrett. You have known Penn Patrick and you have known Walt Disney; you have known Napoleon Hill and your uncle Bucky Fuller; you have known Dr. Edward Deming and Leland Val Van de Wall. Oh yes, you have known a few these many years.

"Our family has been guided in all things by these magical beings, and we have never discussed who it was that crossed your way. For of these great ones, these greatest of all teachers . . . and the chosen MASTERS who mentor each along the 'way'.

"There is another. And this, my son, is the TEACHER of THE MASTERS. . . For the Teacher of the Masters walks this way in life, to pull from the other side of eternity, NEW TRUTH.

"New Truth in each time and space that is required in the moment, to progress life, and to manufacture the way of perfection in God's plan. In any time and place there are so few, so few of these great BEINGS that are alive and which a student's life path may be blessed to cross. And you and I, we have known many ...

"This blessing to us is beyond prayer, and is the finger of God upon our lives. It is a continuous marker from God in the teaching work that I have attempted to deliver to the world. He has confirmed the work through sending me another TEACHER OF MASTERS.

"It is enough.

"More than enough.

"For you see, Bee, the Teacher of the Masters is not appointed by his peers. The Masters do not denote the Teacher of Masters when they appear, for they are eternally KNOWN for who they are by the Masters, the protectors of the truth.

"The Teachers and their Masters have always recognized the Teacher of Masters, as they rarely appear, and provide reverence to them, for the way of their life is a mysterious path.

"And only when a Teacher of Masters comes across their brother Masters on "the path," do they pause to teach, so that their teaching may be made known.

"For if unbidden, unsought, their hidden wisdom remains

silent. And when these few congregate with the others, so that they may hear and know, then from their words, from this, comes the future.

"For the word was made flesh . . .

"And in the beginning, it is a Teacher of Masters, in his or her special KNOWING, who will recognize another Teacher of Masters in the world. In their knowing, it may be years, truly years before that other, so witnessed, is awake enough to know, to gather the force to look within their own surrender, to accept who it is that they truly ARE.

"For their road is impossibly lonely and separate from the road of other men. To accept the burden is to move the transformation forward, once again. Only with enormous courage can such work continue upon the shoulders of mortal men.

"For when the Teacher of Masters speaks his truth, it may be hidden for a long while from the eyes and ears of man. When another such Teacher is recognized by a peer, their nature may rebel and for some time confusion may reign in the life of the newly Witnessed Teacher of Masters.

"However, the soul of the great being may not remain ignorant FOREVER to God's plan, and eventually, in just the right time, the soul will know its true nature. For this is the way of it.

"And now my first-born son . . . it is for you to know . . . that I am dying..." these words spaced painfully between the difficult inhalations . . .

"*I know, Dad.*"

"I won't be coming back now, when I sleep again, Bee . . ."

"*I know, Dad.*"

Squeezing his son's hand, "So I say these words as a man who is dying. To a son who is living and who needs to FEEL these words . . ."

Here he raised his head so his eyes were level with his son's, which took an effort so Herculean, I winced in sympathetic agony.

"Then know that you, my son, ARE a Teacher of Masters, and you have been so for a very long time. And it pains me so, to see you confused by who and what you are. And as I leave you this last time, know that I will NEVER really leave you and that you are among all things to me, MY FOREVER FRIEND. Know that I will take you with me in all ways, and that I will remain beside you in all your days.

"Now, as the father you have well loved, I command you,

to go into the world and discover the true nature of your divine soul, and complete your destiny . . .

"TO TEACH AS A TEACHER OF MASTERS!"

Mr. Dohrmann's eyes closed for the first time, and tears freely flowed as his hands released his son. Bernhard was crying very hard now.

". . .You're my eternal friend too, Dad . . ."

Despite his deep emotion, I could tell that these were still just words to the boy — that it would be a long while before I would see this one learn the last lesson. I took him by the shoulders and walked him down to the family room. Then I returned to sit beside Mr. Dohrmann one last time.

After almost a half hour of labored-breathing nap time, Mr. Dohrmann's hand rose into the air with a finger signaling for me to approach closer.

I came around the bed, still lingering on his words, and the life I had shared with them.

As we sat and stared at one another, I found myself sharing the drinking cup and holding the old master's hands in mine.

"Do you think he has any idea of this last lesson, my friend?"

"No, Alan, it will take some time."

He nodded with a knowing I will always remember. "You have seen all the happy accidents that show themselves to us, Brother Al?"

". . .Yes. So many . . .*SO MANY . . .*"

"It is important that the children remember that when these happy coincidences show up, they are tiny MARKERS FROM GOD. When they are many, it means the way is right and strong. When they are absent for long periods of time, it is meant to mark a hunger. The spirit has to take a risk, and reward the soul with tests that must come one WAY or the other . . . easily and flowing, or challenging and unbidden. But always, the LESSONS will come.

We held hands and communicated our understanding by squeezing.

The Candlelight

~~~~ On the last day, Melissa came downstairs and asked for Bernhard. He was being interviewed by the *Wall Street Journal.* I can remember him saying to the reporter, "I'm sorry, I really must interrupt this now, as my Father is dying."

The other eight children were in the room when Bernhard arrived, and they parted to let him be near their father. The breathing came in great gasps, the bellows of his lungs struggling by pure instinct for the life force that was so strong in him.

He had been asleep now for many days.

The room's shades were drawn and it was dark outside. Twelve candles had been lit; one for each of the nine children, one for Mrs. and Mr. Dohrmann, and one for myself. The candles were placed around Mr. Dohrmann's room in a circle similar to the one that the children made around their father for their lessons.

Bernhard cradled his father in his arms, the teacher's head held to his son's breast as if he were a favorite rag doll.

Everyone held tears and strength at the same time.

And then, a power filled the room; everyone felt it. The nurse who had cared for him for these four years and loved him so, led us in a chant. We asked that he move toward Christ, toward His light, and release all earthly possessions, and that, filled only with our love, he cross into the great light of a higher reality.

Soon after we finished our chant, in three deep but telling breaths that filled his body with racking gasps and filled the room with knowing, he expired. And in the stillness we all could feel POWER rise above the body bag. I remember seeing the children all following with their eyes something that could not be seen. I noticed and reported to my Abbot that the children's faces held an illumination that was far too white and bright for the light of twelve small candles.

When, as if to say, "But, children . . . that's NOT the lesson."

A wind came from *within* the room . . .and each reported it the same way . . . in the same moment . . . all the candles went out.

And the children and their father were in total darkness . . . a final moment . . . together, their faces holding only the illumination from Another Source . . . which was enough to allow us to see one another, filling the room with a soft white glow.

Then, the nurse spoke. She said simply, "WOW!"

As if her words had thrown a switch, the flames instantly returned to all twelve candles. We all watched as the nurse loosened the cradle of Bernhard's arms from his father's head and pulled the sheets over the body bag of an elf that had disappeared.

As Mr. Dohrmann, wrapped in a different, artificial plastic bag, disappeared inside the ambulance, Bernhard said, "That's not him . . .he has gone . . . with the candlelight!"